"Stay with me tonight?" he asked.

Chris's words surprised her, and sent a thrill of hope down Karyn's spine.

"Please," he continued. "Just one more night to make sure my job is complete." His blue eyes smiled down into hers. "I'm not ready for our weekend to end just yet."

Neither was Karyn. But wouldn't spending another night with him just put off the moment she'd have to watch him walk away? After all, they had an agreement. Was she being greedy? Tempting fate? Pleasure blended with misery as the feel of his hand stroking her back made her heart ache and her body hum.

As if sensing her internal debate, Chris leaned across the space between them, persuading her with a deep, sensual kiss. The need for his touch won out over her will, the promise of this moment overruling her fear of the future. "Okay, I'll stay."

He rewarded her with a look that guaranteed her a night she'd never forget.

And that was exactly what she was afraid of....

Blaze™

Dear Reader,

Whispers in the Dark has been a labor of love for me for a very long time. I'm so excited to finally share Chris and Karyn's story with you!

This book began as a question that popped into my head while listening to a lecture on post-traumatic stress disorder. How do you return to a normal life after something tragic happens? For each and every person, just like for Karyn, the answer to that question is different. But the more I wrote, the more I realized determination plays a key part—the same determination we all need in order to tackle the obstacles that block our goals, hopes and dreams. I like to think that Chris and Karyn shared their determination with me. I hope they do the same for you.

I'd love to hear what you think about Chris and Karyn's story. You can contact me at kira@kirasinclair.com or visit me at www.KiraSinclair.com.

Best wishes,

Kira Sinclair

WHISPERS IN THE DARK
Kira Sinclair

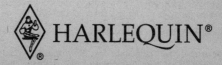

HARLEQUIN®

TORONTO • NEW YORK • LONDON
AMSTERDAM • PARIS • SYDNEY • HAMBURG
STOCKHOLM • ATHENS • TOKYO • MILAN • MADRID
PRAGUE • WARSAW • BUDAPEST • AUCKLAND

ISBN-13: 978-0-373-79419-5
ISBN-10:   0-373-79419-3

WHISPERS IN THE DARK

www.eHarlequin.com

Printed in U.S.A.

ABOUT THE AUTHOR

When not working as an office manager or juggling plotlines, Kira spends her time on a small farm in north Alabama with her wonderful husband, two amazing daughters and a menagerie of animals. While writing in one form or another has always been a part of her life, she's excited to see her first book published with the Harlequin Blaze line. She'd love to hear what you think of her debut, at www.KiraSinclair.com.

There are several people I need to thank, because this book would never have happened without them:

The Playfriends—Andrea, Danniele, Kimberly and Marilyn—for brainstorming, Rumors, teeter-totters, late-night calls and panicked e-mail sessions.

The Mavens—Beverly, LJ and Linda—for setting such a wonderful example.

Rhonda Nelson for that last puzzle piece.

Lori Borrill and Leeanne Kenedy for reading... and reading...and reading again.

Shelley Visconte for the invaluable information.

My own personal hero and our little girls for your love, patience and unflagging support.

And finally, my editor, Brenda, for not giving up on me, Chris or Karyn.

1

"You know, as much as I enjoy this ritual, I'm really starting to resent you hogging my Friday nights."

Karyn Mitchell looked up from her half-painted toes and rolled her eyes at her best friend, Anne. "Funny, I don't remember inviting you, anyway."

"Yeah, well, I know what you'd be doing if I wasn't here…"

"Enjoying a nice, long bath?" Karyn raised a pointed eyebrow.

"Booorrrring." As she flopped down onto the sofa beside Karyn, ice cubes rattled in Anne's fresh drink. "You've been here almost two years—don't you think it's time to see something besides your gray cubicle and the inside of this apartment?"

"I like my apartment." There was nothing wrong with it. Or the fact that she preferred to spend her time safe inside it.

Capping her bottle of Ravished Red, Karyn tried not to let the familiar irritation surface. Anne didn't mean to push. She just couldn't seem to help it.

"And grease-stained pizza boxes and demolished cartons of triple-chocolate meltdown, apparently. But neither of those will help you find a man."

A joking smile crinkled her friend's bright green eyes. It didn't help. This was territory they'd been over before, and Karyn was getting tired of covering the same ground. The only thing that kept her from exploding was the fact that while Anne might appear thick-skinned to the rest of the world, she was really a softie at heart.

"I don't need a man."

Anne snorted, a sound that clashed with her blond, model-quality exterior, but completely suited the rebel she hid inside. "Every woman needs a man, someone to help you feel pretty, feminine…sexy."

"I wouldn't know sexy if it bit me in the ass."

"That's my point." A bright, mischievous smile flashed across Anne's face, lightening Karyn's mood. Anne had that effect on her…on everyone. Sometimes it was sickening. But, God, she'd needed that so much when she'd first moved to Birmingham.

Laughter. Something she'd only faked for years. Her family had smothered her. Cocooned her in bubble wrap and walked on egg shells around her. Even surrounded by people, you could be alone. She just hadn't realized how alone she'd been until she'd met Anne.

It hadn't always been that way. A mischievous child, she'd grown up the center of attention and relished every last moment. And as a teenager, she'd loved being the outgoing, friendly one. Not the most popular girl. But the one everyone turned to for advice and a shoulder to cry on.

Being happy had been easy. Then.

She missed that girl. Wanted her back. It had taken five years, but she was finally starting to find that place inside again. If she could just break through that last barrier to being whole…

"A good man would teach you 'sexy.'" Anne's mouth twisted into an up-to-no-good grin as her eyes flashed fun. "Now turn the radio on. The show's about to start."

Karyn groaned. She had a love/hate relationship with Dr. Desire and his radio show. There was something about that man's voice that made her insides tingle and turn to goo. Listening to him talk about relationships and sex for hours every night drove her crazy. Of course, she supposed it was self-torture, considering she'd given up all hope of ever having sex again.

"You're on the air with Dr. Desire. Let's put some spark back in your love life."

His familiar voice filled the room around her. Calm and pleasant, deep and dark, Dr. Desire had the uncanny ability to put her at ease and hype her up, all with that one catch phrase.

Comfort and confusion, that's what he offered. How could she want everything he talked about—a healthy, satisfying relationship plus sweaty, hedonistic, no-holds-barred sex—and yet still be unable to take that first step in finding it?

Listening to his show had become a nightly ritual, one she shared every Friday with Anne. It had started out as a sort of self-prescribed therapy. She'd hoped that hearing men and women talk about sexual relationships every night would take the edge of fear away, would get her juices flowing again. And it had, it did, but each and every time she'd attempted to put that energy to good use, the anxiety would resurface.

Holy hell, she was frustrated.

She wanted sex. She wanted a life. And she wanted someone to share them both with.

"How can he fulfill your needs if you don't tell him what you want? Listen, ladies, we aren't mind readers. You want a little adventure with your sex? Then spell it out for him. Trust me, he's probably willing to try anything once."

Karyn sighed and leaned back against her sofa. She rattled the ice cubes in her buttery nipple, wishing, not for the first time, that the warm buzz wouldn't go to waste. But she never drank hard liquor in public, not when there were men around to take advantage.

"Call him."

Rolling her head sideways, Karyn shot Anne a glare. "No."

"He'll have the answer."

She stared disbelievingly as Anne hopped up and hobbled across the floor toward the phone.

"Ah, no—he won't."

"Look, how can it hurt? You've seen how many therapists over the last few years?"

"Four in five years."

"And has anything they've told you to do helped?"

"No."

"Precisely." Anne duck-walked back to protect her wet polish. With a raised eyebrow and cocked hip, she thrust out the handset. "What do you have to lose?"

Staring at the thing like it was a mud-covered spider, Karyn said, "Uh, my dignity, self-respect, sanity? Any of those will work. There is no way I'm going on the most popular radio show in the city to spill my guts. Everyone I know listens to this show. You're the only person here who knows what happened. I plan to keep it that way."

"So lie, use a different name. No one will know."

"I'll know."

"You're assuming he can't help—"

"He can't. You listen to the show just as much as I do. He might know a heck of a lot about the male/female thing, but somehow I think my problems run a bit deeper than the normal issues he handles. I do not need a sex expert."

"That man is an expert on more than just sex. He knows how to handle a woman, make her feel special. Although, if you ask me, a sexpert is precisely what you need."

Anne frowned and Karyn thought, *Oh, shit.* Her best friend bright and animated…that was normal. Her best friend with a mission…that was just scary.

"That man could charm the panties off anyone—including you. He'd have you naked and panting before fears and your overactive brain could sabotage you."

Standing up, Karyn paced past her friend toward the stereo. She should just turn the damn thing off. Instead she turned back and asked, "What do you think he's going to say?"

Anne lifted one challenging brow. "It's more what I expect he could *do*."

"Do? What, you think he'll pimp for me? Find a man willing to take on the challenge?"

Anne twirled the phone in her hand. "Nope. I expect he'd help you himself if you asked."

Her knees went weak, almost like someone had reached in and pulled the bones straight through the bottom of her feet. "Asked. You expect me to ask Dr. Desire for sex?"

"Hell, yes."

"Hell, no."

"He's precisely what you need. He definitely knows his way around a woman's body. Any man who can talk about women and pleasure the way he does…" Her friend trailed off into a wistful sigh. "At least call him."

Karyn shook her head, not sure what to say. There was no way she could ask Dr. Desire for sex. On air no less!

Narrowing her eyes, Anne jabbed the phone toward her. "If you don't, I will."

Karyn's heart seemed to seize in her chest. Pulling her gaze away, she decided to ignore the pointed gesture.

Anne shrugged and started dialing.

Snatching the phone from her, midpunch, she stabbed the off button and hid it behind her back.

With a smirk Anne said, "I have a cell phone, you know."

Karyn growled under her breath. Arguing with Anne made

her almost as frustrated as fighting with her big brothers always had. A tiny part of her missed those moments with her family, when she could be herself, when her older brothers had acted like annoying, interfering older brothers. No one except Anne fought with her now.

"Look, I'm not asking that man to sleep with me."

"Fine. But call him. It can't hurt to tell him your story, see if he has any advice."

Karyn swayed. Sure, she'd considered calling before. The only thing that had stopped her was an absolute certainty that it wouldn't do any good.

Crossing the room, Anne laid a hand on her shoulder. "You've tried everything else. What do you have to lose?"

She gave up with an exasperated groan. "What am I supposed to say to him? Hi, my name is Karyn and I'm a victim of rape?"

"Well, that depends on what you're looking for. I'd suggest you start with the fact you haven't had sex in five years and go from there."

Plopping down onto her sofa, Karyn dialed the number for Dr. Desire's hot line, 1-800-4DESIRE and cringed. It sounded a little too close to a phone-sex line for her peace of mind. But if this would get Anne off her back for a while it'd be worth any discomfort. She'd call, tell him her problem and just see if he had any suggestions.

What she wouldn't do was ask him for sex.

Her heartbeat quickened as the line connected and rang. The bundle of nerves in the pit of her stomach seemed to tighten and churn as she explained to the show's producer why she was calling.

After being placed on hold, Karyn breathed deeply in a vain attempt to dispel the emotions jittering through her. She'd explain her situation—leaving out most of the details—and then when he couldn't offer her anything constructive would hang up and forget she'd ever dialed the number.

She felt better, until she looked up into her friend's expectant eyes.

"I still think you should ask him for sex. I'm telling you, that man knows his way around a woman's body. The only thing you'd be thinking with him touching you is more, more, more."

The breathless way Anne moaned the words was not helping. "I am not going—"

"You're on the air with Dr. Desire. Let's find the spark in your relationship."

Karyn's eyes flew wide as she leaped to her feet, standing uselessly in the center of her living room. His voice slid down her spine, not from her strategically placed speakers, but from the phone pressed tightly to her ear. Her hand flexed around the curved plastic in a bid to hold on to something tight. She certainly didn't have hold of her sanity at the moment.

A vision of Dr. Desire, a carbon copy of the billboard she passed at least twice a day, jumped easily to her mind.

With a wide, white smile and rumpled, dark brown hair that always looked as if some woman had just run her fingers through it, the man was gorgeous. No red-blooded, breathing woman could argue that. But it wasn't just his rugged jaw or kissable lips that held her attention. Something deep inside those smoldering blue-gray eyes made her insides clench and melt whenever she drove past.

Even now, just the memory of that picture had her body heating. Heating more than it had for any flesh-and-blood man in the past five years.

"Now, don't be shy. I won't bite. Unless you want me to."

Karyn heard his laugh. Like his voice, it was deep and sexy and somehow soothing. She relaxed the muscles that had bunched at her back and sank blindly onto the sofa.

Her mouth opened and words tumbled out before she could stop them.

"I need you to sleep with me."

CHRISTOPHER FAULKNER nearly fell off his chair. He did bobble the microphone in front of him.

Considering the timid way this woman had started her phone call, that last statement had been a shocker.

Jerking up, he mouthed, "What the hell," to Michael, his forty-two-year-old producer. The man supposedly screening his calls just shrugged and went back to playing with switches.

Chris fought down the urge to strangle him. He'd wrangled with that sensation often over their five-year friendship. There was something about the other man's laid-back attitude that tended to grate against his nerves. Especially during the past few months.

Michael knew he didn't like to deal with this sort of thing on air. Hell, he could barely walk out his door without being accosted by some primped-up prima donna looking for him to rock her world. All they ever really wanted was an instant catapult to notoriety. Or money.

The novelty of fame had long since lost its shine. He really enjoyed helping people, but could have done without some of the headaches that went with the job.

Pasting a smile on his face—because the listeners really could hear when it wasn't there—he put every ounce of experience he'd gained over the past five years into handling the thorny situation Michael had dropped in his lap.

At least he'd learned something on his journey from ordinary nighttime DJ to megastar.

"Well, gee, I'm flattered." He forced out a laugh that fell as flat as the lie he'd just told. He was nowhere close to being flattered. In fact, he was much closer to annoyed.

"That's not… I didn't mean… Let me explain."

The young woman's voice floated into his ears through the headphones he wore. He heard desperation, which scared him, but also something underneath that caught his attention. Something sweet with a tinge of the same uneasiness he was trying to ignore. In a strange way it stirred a connection, a sense of kinship with the woman on the other end.

"I know this must sound crazy to you and, frankly, I wouldn't blame you if you cut me off, but please just hear me out. Honestly, I didn't mean what I said before. Really."

Her admission took a bit of the edge off. Barely.

She paused, sucking in air. The broken sound reverberated through his brain. When she started again her voice trembled and he wondered what had made her take this step. Whatever she was trying to say, it was obviously difficult.

"My name is Katy." Her voice faltered and drifted away for a moment before beginning again. "This is hard for me to talk about."

"Well, I can't say I'll sleep with you, Katy." He forced out another laugh, but even he could hear the brittle edge. "But I'd like to help. Tell me what's going on."

"About five years ago I was date raped. I knew the guy. Not very well, but enough to think I'd be safe with him. I wasn't."

A tight knot dropped into his stomach, punching straight through to his toes.

How had this girl gotten through? She'd already hit two of the auto-dump buttons—propositioning him and having a serious sexual issue, one that required professional help. He was no professional.

His unfinished business-management degree didn't really qualify him to deal with severe sexual hang-ups. And if, in the silence of his own mind, he'd thought once or twice about remedying that deficiency in his education…well, there'd never been a reason to admit that idiocy to anyone.

He stared hard through the glass at Michael. The other man's forehead was wrinkled even more than usual. Sure, now he cared. Where had that interest been five minutes ago?

Katy's voice continued, tightening and turning to an emotionless monotone while she recited the bare-bones facts he really didn't want to hear.

"It was terrifying and a long time ago. But I can't seem to move past it. I've tried so many things, listened to so many people. No one seems to have the answer."

"The answer to what?" The sound of his own voice coming through the headphones shocked him. Why had he asked her that?

"I can't have sex. I want to." The girl groaned softly, the sound lodging right next to the knot at the bottom of his stomach. "God, I want to. But even thinking about it—I freeze up."

His eyes locked with Michael's through the pane of glass between them, narrowing to slits. His jaw clamped so tight he thought the entire audience could probably hear the grinding sound.

This girl had a serious problem. Not the "my boyfriend won't go down on me," "my girlfriend won't do a threesome," "is this burning sensation something to worry about" kind of stuff he dealt with in a normal night. She needed some professional help. She did not need him.

This had disaster written all over it. His show was bubble-gum and handcuffs, not emotional turmoil.

He'd fallen into the job as Dr. Desire. A few comments to a late-night caller and before he knew it, what had been a play-the-records, punch-the-buttons kind of job had turned into hours of sex and relationship discussions that led to more than he'd ever imagined. But he'd worked hard over the past five years to build a public persona, to provide confidence and helpful information to those seeking sexual answers and a push to try something new.

The people who called into his show—the people that got past Michael's supposed screening process—mostly wanted relationship advice or to share their own fantasies or be turned on.

He was prepared for that. He was not prepared for this.

"Katy, as much as I'd like to help you, I'm not a doctor. It sounds to me like you need to see a professional."

"I've talked to a therapist. Four, in fact. None of them helped."

He looked again at Michael, raising his hands in the universal sign for "What the hell do I do now?"

His producer's response was the cut sign—a hand across his throat. He'd like nothing better than to end this call, but he didn't think that would be a very good idea. Not for Katy. And certainly not for the show. His female listeners—who comprised more than half his audience—would raise hell. How could he extract himself without appearing cold and indifferent?

"Well, Katy. Maybe you just need to give yourself some more time. You had to have been young. You barely sound old enough to drink." He pushed out another laugh, trying to maintain the tone of the show despite feeling stuck between a rock and a hard place.

"I'm twenty-six and it hasn't gotten any better in five years. That's a long time. I want a husband and kids. At the rate I'm going I'll be fifty before I have sex again." Another desperate sound echoed across the line and twanged the nerves at the bottom of his spine. "I don't think I could handle that."

"I'm sure that's not true. You'll have sex when you're ready. I have to ask—" although something told him he'd be better off if he didn't "—what makes you think you'd be any different with me?"

"I honestly didn't mean to say that. But I've been listening to your show for a long time and it's obvious you know what you're talking about. Maybe that's what I need, a man who really understands how to give a woman pleasure. Who knows how to ignore the fear."

Chris shifted in his seat, completely surprised that the quivery little dip in her voice there at the end had caught his attention.

"You should never ignore the fear, Katy. Listen to your body, it knows what you can handle."

Chris paused, leaning in closer to the mike. He really wanted to help this woman, but he couldn't, not without risking everything he'd built. His show walked a line between offering professional-sounding advice and providing an opinion. Chris tried hard to stay far away from that line. One toe over could cost him everything. One lawsuit because he'd said the wrong thing to the wrong person... Katy was just too close to that edge for comfort.

"I know you understand I can't sleep with you, but please find another therapist. Maybe this time his or her suggestions will work. The fact you were willing to call into the show tells me how important this is for you and how much you're willing to risk to get what you want. You don't need me. You need to trust yourself. Find a nice man who'll understand and go slowly with you. If you need the number of a therapist, stay on the line, and I'll get the information for you."

"Thank you."

He'd expected her voice to waver or maybe crack with disappointment. It didn't. In fact, she seemed almost, well, relieved.

"ARE YOU HAPPY NOW? I made a complete ass of myself in front of half the south."

"Sure you did...Katy." Anne winked before hobbling to the kitchen and coming back with a half-empty bottle of butterscotch schnapps. "No one but me knows that was you on the radio."

"And it better stay that way."

Anne smiled. "Of course."

Karyn fought the urge to say something snide to wipe the expression off her face. Her friend hadn't done anything wrong. She'd been the idiot who'd called and blurted out a request for sex.

"You know, I never would have said that if you hadn't been pounding at me about how perfect he would be as my sex stud."

Pouring another drink, Anne looked over the edge of her glass. "I think you said exactly what you wanted to. Not that it matters."

"Oh, it matters."

"Besides, I happen to agree with him."

"What? You're the one who told me to sleep with him—"

"Not about that. I think you need to find a man, Karyn. One who understands what you've gone through. One who'll go slow and take things one step at a time."

Karyn paced to her bookshelf and back. Realizing she still held the phone in her hand, she tossed it away in disgust. What? Did they all think she was stupid? Of course that was what she needed.

"Absolutely. And a guy like that isn't hard to find. Because telling a man on the first date that there won't be any sex in his foreseeable future due to the fact that I'm a rape survivor really turns men on."

"So, don't tell him."

Turning to her friend, Karyn cocked her head to the side and stared. "You're the one who said I need to find a man who understands. Kinda hard to do if I don't tell him."

"So, just not on the first date."

Karyn sank down onto the couch. Tears of frustration pricked the backs of her eyes. "That doesn't work either because then I spend the entire night worrying about what he expects and how I'll handle it."

"Fine, be miserable." Anne slipped down beside her on the edge of the sofa and wrapped a supportive arm around her shoulders. "But nothing's going to change, Karyn, until you take a chance."

2

"WE HAVE TO DO something."

Chris's voice echoed against the impersonal walls of the station conference room. He sat in the padded seat to Michael's right and looked across at the two gentlemen he'd asked to join them, the station manager and their attorney.

"We agree. The entire show was dominated by calls about Katy for the third day in a row. Even though your ratings are up this can't continue. If we take no action there will be a backlash against the show eventually. Your listeners want and expect you to do something."

"Something we all know I can't do." Chris leaned over the gleaming surface of the conference table and studied the two men opposite him. To him they resembled aging bulldogs with their sagging faces. They walked around, their mouths pulled down into perpetual frowns as if their every decision affected the balance of the world.

Only, today their decisions affected him.

He hadn't felt this out of control in years. Yes, he had money, fast cars and a house he owned outright and had remodeled with his own two hands. But it was his show that was his security and stability. And at the moment, that security felt more like a smoke screen than something solid. If the show ended, he had nothing to fall back on. The Dr. Desire gig had landed in his lap. That kind of miracle wasn't likely to happen twice.

Which was why he normally kept a tight rein on his life and his show. But sometime in the past two days he'd lost that control. With or without the agreement of the men before him, he'd do whatever he needed to get it back. Chris never again wanted to experience the sickening sense of helplessness he had at sixteen when he and his mother had been evicted. One random, unfair event—her illness and inability to work—had cost them everything.

He would never be that vulnerable, that dependant, again.

Michael chimed in. "The listeners will eventually become less concerned and more forceful. And while I normally wouldn't worry, we've just moved into several major markets. If our ratings begin to slip we're liable to lose them as fast as we gained them."

Chris's stomach clenched for one brief moment at the thought before he pushed it away. That wasn't going to happen. "Michael is right. We need to do something, but I'll be damned if I know what. I obviously can't have sex with her."

The attorney's face flushed hot before returning to its regular mottled red. "Absolutely not. In fact, I'd advise against it."

"What if I took her out to dinner? A nice, impersonal meal. She said she hadn't been on a date in a while. That would help in one area without moving us into dangerous territory."

Three sets of eyebrows shot straight up, but he watched as they all rolled the thought around and considered.

"It might work." Michael spoke first, his enthusiasm for the idea gaining ground. "It would be a chance for her to meet you face-to-face, you could charm her, give her a T-shirt, CD. At the same time it would give us the opportunity to make a statement on air, something to the effect that we're doing everything we can to help."

Looking questioningly at Ken, Chris waited.

The attorney spoke slowly, weighing things out as he went. "We'd need to keep the details from your listeners. A simple announcement that you heard their concerns and that we're getting Katy the help she needs. For her protection, you can't reveal specifics, but want to assure everyone that you and the station are committed to helping this bright young woman through a traumatic experience."

Despite having made the suggestion, Chris wasn't entirely convinced it was the best idea. In fact, he wasn't exactly sure where it had come from.

Certainly, he'd taken female listeners to dinner before. More than he cared to count over the past five years actually. At first he'd enjoyed the attention Dr. Desire received from the female population. He'd wanted sex, and the women had wanted a brush with fame. Everyone had walked away satisfied. But lately, satisfaction hadn't been enough.

Obviously, this would be different. He wouldn't expect sex when the night was done, and he would make it clear to Katy that that wasn't his intention—for her sake, as well as his.

He turned the idea over one more time, examining it for pitfalls. If eating a simple meal with her allowed him to lose the sense of guilt he'd been fighting for the past few days, got his audience off his back and helped Katy, well, then maybe it would be worth a few hours out of his life.

Heath, the station manager, jumped in as devil's advocate. "Couldn't we simply say that without actually doing anything? I mean, we did offer her information on therapists."

Ken countered immediately, "Certainly, if we could guarantee Katy won't come forward to discredit the statement. If that happened, the show and the station would look worse than you already do."

Chris pushed up from the table, walked to the floor-to-ceiling glass windows and looked out over Birmingham's skyline. Ruffling a hand through his hair, he could feel the tight pinch of a headache coming on.

"We don't know how to get in touch with her, that's certainly a problem."

Papers rustled behind his back before Heath said, "We had her call-in number traced. We have her real name, address and home telephone number."

Chris turned and stared at the station manager before moving his gaze to the attorney.

"Is that even legal?"

Ken shifted in his chair, but met Chris's ice-blue stare. "It's a bit gray, but nothing that could land anyone in jail."

"Isn't that a relief." Chris narrowed his eyes, boring holes into the other man.

"You should do it, Chris. It's the best way out of this. One night from your life and it's over. Charm the pan—" Michael stalled and cleared his throat. "Charm her a little. Piece of cake for Dr. Desire."

The impish grin he gave rubbed Chris the wrong way. But whatever Michael's faults—and they were many—the man did have his back when it mattered. At the moment he was making it difficult to remember that but…

Taking Katy out for a nice dinner would be simple for Dr. Desire. Chris on the other hand…he wasn't convinced. She'd expect him to be *on,* they all did. Smooth, sexy, sophisticated. Intelligent. Funny. Perfect.

Most women wanted everything from a man. Unfortunately, he'd done his job so well they all seemed to think he could give that to them. He was tired of trying. Tired of pretending that the persona he'd built was real.

One night out of his life.

"I'll call her. But if she doesn't want to do this, we all agree to issue a statement on air, anyway."

"Agreed."

Chris took the paper Ken held out to him and glanced down at the neat black ink against the white page.

"Karyn Mitchell." He liked that much better than Katy.

KARYN WALKED into her apartment, threw her keys onto the hall table and hung her purse and briefcase on the coatrack. Walking into the silent kitchen, she couldn't hold back a sigh.

Her head pounded, her shoulders slumped and a brick seemed to have lodged at the base of her spine. She knew stress, tension and exhaustion were responsible for her weary state.

It had been four days since that damn phone call. For the past three nights she'd turned on Dr. Desire only to hear his show become a heated discussion of her life and what he should do to help her.

Her hours at work hadn't even been safe. Every time she'd tried to add up a string of numbers today someone had popped their head into her cubicle to gossip about Katy.

Her so-called best friend hadn't been much better. Anne had teased and admonished, going so far as to try to cajole her into a double date. After hours of frustration Karyn had snapped at her. And felt guilty for it afterward.

But the frustration and anger hadn't lasted long. It was hard to keep her bad mood when Anne was around. She was always so…chipper. Or rather, that's what she showed the world. Even Karyn hadn't realized that the brightness and light Anne seemed surrounded with was a facade. Not until it had slipped. She'd truly known they were friends the night Anne had broken down and allowed her to see the emotions she buried deep inside.

That same night Karyn had opened up and shared her own deepest secret. She'd never regretted the action or the trust she'd placed in the other woman.

At the moment, however, she *was* seriously regretting sharing that secret with half the South, even if she had used an alias.

She couldn't believe it was happening all over again. She'd moved to Birmingham to get away from this kind of minute dissection of her life and choices. She'd spent years defending her actions to newspapers, TV stations, radio shows, her lawyers, the judge, not to mention the jury.

The job offer from Walker Technologies had provided her with a clean start, the chance to lose herself in the city crowds and forget the trauma everyone at home remembered when they looked at her. And with one five-minute phone conversation she'd inadvertently opened herself up to it all over again.

The one saving grace was that the city was discussing *Katy's* life, not hers. But she wondered how long that would last. Reporters had a way of digging up details, especially the ones you thought safe and secret. Unfortunately, the only thing she could do was wait and hope the interest died down soon. Doing anything else would just draw attention to herself.

She'd gone in to work this morning hoping to bury herself in the minutia of number crunching. It hadn't worked—she'd completely screwed up the monthly sales report and it had taken all afternoon to rework it. She'd become an accountant because she loved numbers, because they followed hard-and-fast rules that never changed. Today she wasn't so enamored of them or her job.

If only people hadn't kept interrupting her. If only she'd been able to concentrate on the numbers instead of Dr. Desire…

There was no escape. She kept telling herself that the interest in Katy would die down eventually, that something else would happen to catch everyone's attention.

At the moment, that wasn't very comforting; what would be was a hot bath, a good book and a glass of wine. The only food she wanted was a tub of mint chocolate chip ice cream covered in fudge sauce. Comfort and solitude at its finest. She'd pay for it tomorrow at the gym, but it would be so worth it.

Opening the freezer, she pulled out the half-empty carton and grabbed a spoon. With a hip bump she closed the spoon drawer and headed into the bathroom to start her night of relaxation.

Pouring the wine, picking out her book and turning on some soft music all helped her settle. She slipped into the hot water with an appreciative sigh. The last of the stress that had built inside melted away with the rising steam. Closing her eyes, she rested her head and just sat for a minute, soaking up a luxury she rarely made time for.

After a few minutes of bliss, she reached for the ice cream and scooped a bite from the carton, letting the cold glob melt in her mouth and slip down her throat. The bold, heavy taste burst through her mouth, reminding her of the mint tea her grandmother had always made on sticky summer days when she'd visited.

Times like these she missed her family, even her mother. Yes, she'd needed to escape Darby, Mississippi, to put some space between her family's overprotective tendencies and her mother's inability to understand. It had been an important step in her recovery, one she'd needed to take.

The anonymity she'd found in Birmingham hadn't hurt, either. Closing her eyes, she tried to ignore the feeling that it was slowly slipping away.

She'd just scooped another heaping spoonful into her mouth when the phone rang. Reaching for the cordless she'd brought into the bathroom, she looked at the caller ID and groaned. She should have known better than to bring the phone into her haven of solitude.

Pounding the button, she answered, knowing if she didn't her brother would send up a hue and cry to the entire family.

"Hello, Blake."

"Hi, squirt, how's it going?"

She couldn't suppress the smile just hearing his voice caused. "Well, I was enjoying some downtime until you called. How can I convince you to get lost?"

"You can't. I'm the official family envoy. If I don't go back to Mom and Dad with specific information, we're both likely to regret it."

And wasn't that the truth? Growing up the youngest of three kids and being the only girl meant she was very protected as a child and teenager. If her parents hadn't worried about something, her older brothers sure had. It'd been a miracle that any guy had wanted to date her. Outgoing and confident, she'd been so eager to escape to college.

The overprotective atmosphere had only gotten worse after she'd been raped. It was her family's natural response, to circle the wagons and ward off anything else that could hurt her. And at the time, she'd appreciated their love and understanding. But it had gotten old awfully fast and was the main reason she'd placed a state between her and the rest of the Mitchell clan.

With a sigh of resignation she said, "Okay. What do they want?"

"You to visit. We haven't seen you since Christmas. That's seven months, in case you've lost the ability to count along with the ability to find your way home."

Karyn settled back into the steaming water, letting her hand play back and forth making waves. This would not end quickly, she could tell.

"I can't get away from work right now." And the thought of going back to Darby always left her slightly unsettled. The place held memories she'd been trying so hard to leave behind. She might not have been raped there, but she'd certainly gone back to live through the aftermath. The long wait, the trial, the media coverage, then the subsequent realization that her word hadn't been enough for twelve of her peers.

She'd worked so hard to get her life back. And aside from this one last major hurdle—her inability to relax and trust someone enough to have sex—she was doing pretty well. But the thought of returning right now left a sour taste in her mouth.

Not to mention how the family couldn't stop treating her like the wounded baby sister. Whether they meant to or not, they always seemed to reinforce her feelings of self-doubt and fear. The same emotions she was trying hard to shed so that she could move on with her life.

There had been a time when she'd been confident, invincible. She really wanted to find her way back to that woman.

"Look, Karyn, I understand why coming home is hard for you, but everyone only worries more when they don't see or hear from you for a while."

Everyone worried even when they did, so she didn't see what difference it made. And while she understood their reactions, they hadn't helped her much.

"The rest of us are getting together for Labor Day, a nice family picnic on the lake."

"I'll see what I can do, but I make no promises."

"I'm sure you have no concern for the messenger, but I'll pass that along. And don't be surprised when you get a call from Mom."

Oh, she wouldn't. "I still owe you payback for a few childhood incidents. I'll let you handle Mama."

He gave a derisive snort and paused for a moment before his voice went deep with concern. "I worry about you, sis. I know I probably shouldn't, but I can't help it. I've been watching out for you for twenty-six years."

"I'm fine. I'll try to get away. Tell Mom, Dad and Randall that I love them."

"Will do, squirt."

Before she could hang up, the familiar guilt crept in. "I love you, too, Blake. I know you're just trying to help and I appreciate your concern."

"Yeah, well, what are brothers for?"

"You mean besides torturing me as a child and tormenting me as a teenager?"

She heard his laugh resonate down the line before it went dead. Placing the phone on the edge of the tub, she settled back to resume her evening of self-pampering. At least as much of it as she could get in before her mother called.

Which was why when the phone rang again twenty minutes later, Karyn barely looked up from the book she'd been reading. Answering without glancing at the caller ID—there was no need—she said, "I'm fine. I'll try to be there for Labor Day but I make no promises. Give my love to everyone. Bye."

She'd moved the phone away, not wanting to give her mother a chance to talk her into chatting—she'd call back tomorrow or on the weekend maybe—when a single word stopped her dead.

"Wait."

The small sound echoed from the receiver. That was definitely not her mother's voice—unless she'd developed a severe case of laryngitis.

Looking at the caller ID didn't help; it showed Unknown.

"Hello?" The tiny sound reverberated out of the receiver.

Karyn nearly dropped the phone into the water. That voice sounded strangely familiar. Almost like… No. It couldn't be.

There was one way to find out. Holding the phone gingerly by two fingers, she put it to her ear, said, "Hello?" and held her breath.

"Karyn? This is Christopher Faulkner."

Oh my God. It was. Her book slid from numb fingers, landing with a liquid plop before swishing beneath the bathwater. Why was Dr. Desire calling her? And how had he gotten her number, her name for that matter?

She closed her eyes, a blush of embarrassment joining the flush on her skin from the heat. She did not want to talk to this man.

"Karyn?"

Dread sloshed through her body. She couldn't stop the knee-jerk reaction to cover herself and cringed as a wave of water splashed over the side of the tub, soaking the deep green mat on the floor.

"Why are you calling?" She knew the urge to rush for her robe was idiotic, but that didn't stop her from leaning against the cold acrylic to shield her naked body with the edge of the tub.

"Do you know who I am?"

A tingle rippled down her back, goose bumps following the path. She told herself the reaction was from the cool air across her wet skin.

Did she know who he was? Oh, she knew all right.

"Yes."

Pulling her legs up under her, she glanced across the room to her towel hanging on the rod by the door. Getting it would mean standing up. Standing up would mean a rush of water, something he would surely hear. For some reason she didn't want him to know how naked—and vulnerable—she was.

"Great. I'm calling to ask you out to dinner."

Whatever she'd expected, that had not been it.

"You what? Why?"

"I want to help. And while sex with you is out of the question, maybe a dinner date might move you in the right direction."

The right direction? Karyn bit back a bitter laugh. At the moment she wasn't even sure where that was.

Dinner. How in heaven's name did he think that would help her sexual frustration and inability to trust anyone with her body?

"What's in this for you?"

"I'd like to make an announcement on the show, nothing specific, just a quick mention that we're getting you help."

An attempt to control the unruly mess his show had turned into over the last few days. Maybe if she agreed to this, the fervor over Katy would die down and the entire city would stop talking about her life.

"Why don't you just say that, anyway? We both know you don't really want to do this."

Silence echoed across the line. Karyn wondered where he was. At the station, in his home, naked in his own bed? Screwing her eyes tightly shut, she wiped that mental image right from her brain. At the station. Definitely. His show would start in an hour or so.

"Look, *Katy,* I have a reputation to uphold. I won't go on air and lie to my listeners."

"I won't tell."

"Yes, but I'll know."

Her mouth opened to tell him, not a snowball's chance in hell, but she couldn't force the words out. A few hours from her life. A chance to put the entire situation behind her and maybe get his listeners to do the same. One night had the potential to wipe the slate clean, almost turn back time.

"Fine. But no media. No publicity. I don't want anyone to know who I am."

"Agreed."

Her heart sped up, not with concern, but excitement.

"I'll meet you at Masquerade Saturday night at seven. Do you know where it is?"

"Sure." She didn't, but she'd figure it out.

"Well, then, I'll see you in a couple days."

Karyn shifted sideways, forgetting about the waist-high water she sat in.

He chuckled, the deep, light sound tickling her heightened senses. "Enjoy your bath."

Unexpected heat melted through her. She cringed, but before she could make a snappy recovery, he hung up, leaving her dangling.

Flopping back into the water, Karyn closed her eyes and flung an arm across her flaming face. "I'm such an idiot."

3

"EVERYTHING'S SET?" Michael met Chris at the door, pushing back a throng of women to let him into Oxygen, a downtown Birmingham hotspot. These personal appearances were part of the job, but he really wished the marketing department would find someplace other than local clubs and bars. The place reeked of smoke, and the pounding music and flashing lights made it difficult to carry on a conversation. Although, sometimes that worked in his favor.

"We're meeting for dinner Saturday night. I reserved a private room at Masquerade."

"Private, huh? Please tell me you aren't considering making a move. I know you've been off your dating game lately, but that's low."

Chris frowned. He was not off his game; he was out of it entirely. But that was by choice. He was tired of pasting on a smile and playing someone else, someone he no longer wanted to be.

"Of course not. I'm trying to keep a low profile. Somewhere I can get in and out without anyone noticing me."

"Dr. Desire! Dr. Desire!" Two women slipped past the bruiser holding back the crowd and raced toward him, yelling at the top of their lungs. Chris took a bracing step backward and held his breath. Before they could reach him, another security guard provided by the club intercepted them.

With a wry twist of lips Michael said, "I wouldn't count on it."

"Those women knew I'd be here." Shaking his head, he moved across the room. "I promised Katy no publicity. No pictures, no interviews. And no using her real name on the air."

His producer shrugged. "Fine. Legal wanted as much, anyway."

"Great. Make sure everyone knows. The last thing I need is for this meeting to leak out. Then Katy really would have something to complain about."

Chris settled into the uncomfortable chair set behind a table at one end of the dark room. Glancing down at the stack of glossy black-and-whites, he suppressed a cringe. He hated autographing these pictures, but they were part of the personal-appearance contract he'd signed.

The man staring back was familiar, but not someone he recognized as himself. The concealing layers were visible, at least to him. Slicked-back, styled hair. False, white smile. Tailored suit, a carbon copy of the straining shoulder seams he now shrugged uncomfortably against.

He'd worked hard to develop Dr. Desire's public persona. The fact that it didn't quite fit hadn't always bothered him. But it was starting to more and more.

"Dr. Desire." A middle-aged woman stepped up to the table and leaned across to squeeze his neck like they were old friends. It was time to go to work.

He spent the next hour talking and laughing with his fans. His cheek muscles hurt from the perpetual smiling, and his throat could have used about five gallons of water.

Of all the things that came along with being Dr. Desire, the public appearances had become his least favorite.

Finally, just at the point he was seriously beginning to think his wrist would fall off, Michael spoke to the crowd. "Sorry, folks. Dr. Desire has to get back to the station. But be sure to check out the Web site for his next local appearance."

With a smile he could no longer feel, Chris waved as he slipped back out the door. Several feet down the block, his shoulders rose and fell on a sigh of relief.

"Remind me not to agree to another one of these for at least six months."

"Sorry, you're doing another in two weeks."

Rolling his stiff neck, Chris let out a groan.

"Publicity means money, for you and the station. Wait here for me. I need to check on something inside, then you can give me a ride back to the station."

When had he become a damn taxi? Whatever. It gave him a few minutes of solitude to unwind. These things always drained him. It was weird, the difference between speaking on air and speaking in person. The people were often the same; at least, they all wanted to talk about the same things. But at night, after the show ended and he left the studio behind, he was never as exhausted as he was after these in-your-face appearances.

Chris walked farther away, knowing that the bouncers who'd held the crowd back would soon let them go. Late-summer heat waved up from the pavement at his feet. Even an hour after sunset it still held every ounce of the August sun. But there was a nice, unusual breeze. It slipped past him, carrying the smells of the city.

Birmingham was nothing like the little Alabama town he'd come from. Back home the smell on the breeze would have been cow manure, freshly mown grass or a mixture of both. It would have held the mouthwatering scents of barbecuing meat and roasting corn, though neither of those would ever have been coming from his own trailer. Here he just smelled money, concrete and the Chinese place down the block. Not necessarily bad, just different.

"Chris."

He turned instinctively, realizing too late that the smooth voice was not Michael's.

Every muscle in his body froze. His skin flushed hot before going clammy cold. He hadn't seen his father for fourteen years. In fact, he'd only laid eyes on the man once in his life.

As far as he was concerned, that was once too many.

"How are you, son?" With a blinding smile that reminded Chris a little too much of the pictures he'd just signed, Darrell Odom cuffed him on the shoulder in greeting.

Shock quickly gave way to a bone-clenching anger. The one time he and his mother had needed the sorry son of a bitch, he had laughed in their faces and told his mother she was a stupid piece of ass for getting herself in trouble in the first place.

"What do you want?" He bit out each precise word. Every cell in his body screamed at him to take the shot he'd wanted to all his life, to pummel the perfect white teeth, golden tanned face and bright blue eyes until they were an unrecognizable mass. He wouldn't, his mama had taught him better. And if he did he'd be no better than his father.

As far as Chris was concerned, he wanted nothing from the man, especially not the questionable moral compass he seemed to operate by.

"Can't a father say hello to his son?"

"Not you. Let me guess, your latest mark wised up and threw you out on your ass." Chris smiled. A small spot in the center of his chest warmed as his father's jaw clenched, confirming his suspicions. "She catch you with another woman or just in your lies?"

Darrell's smile vanished. The change was remarkable. The jovial, polished man he'd been two seconds ago was replaced by someone Chris never would have recognized in a crowd. For the first time he wondered just how old his father actually was. He'd never asked his mother.

Ripples of lines bracketed the man's drawn lips. Deep furrows creased his forehead and the healthy glow he'd radiated vanished to a pale shadow of what it had been before.

"Fine. You're an adult now—"

Like the man had ever known him as a child.

"The bitch I was with threw me out without a cent. No warning, no nothing, just changed the locks. I don't even have a spare set of clothes. I just need enough to get back on my feet, to get a place to stay, some clothes to wear. Ten thousand should do it."

Chris's body flushed hot, and a shot of adrenaline coursed into his veins. He'd been waiting for this day all his life. He'd often railed at God and fate for what had happened to his mother. She'd worked so hard, spent every moment of her life paying for a mistake no one had loved her enough to forgive.

He'd carried the weight of knowing that mistake had been him. And that no matter how perfect a child he'd been, how excellent a student, he couldn't save her. In the end he'd watched as cancer had eaten her from the inside out, knowing that if she'd had a better, easier life—some insurance—that life might have lasted longer.

Now the man who could have helped them and had refused was standing with his own hand out. Life was cruel. But fate had a sense of humor.

A harsh laugh that Chris didn't recognize as his own echoed through the falling night. "Let me get this straight—I watched that night as you denied I was your son, as you told my mother she was an idiot for not aborting me and that any messes she'd made were hers to clean up. You refused to give us even $500 and here you are asking for twenty times that. You're joking, right?"

Darrell's face turned deep red beneath his too-perfect tan. "I know you have it. I didn't have five hundred to spare."

"You mean your sugar mama wouldn't give money to the mother of your bastard son. You make me sick. You're not getting a penny from me."

Chris turned to leave, rubbing at his chest to ease the tight band there. Somehow that hadn't felt as good as he'd always assumed it would.

Staccato steps on the empty sidewalk alerted Chris that the moment wasn't over just yet.

"Don't you walk away from me, boy."

Darrell grabbed at his arm, but Chris was too quick. He spun around, stepping into the man to stop him short.

His father's blue eyes glowed with an ominous heat. "Your mother should have taught you manners, *son.*"

"Don't you mention her to me, you bastard. *Ever.* You don't know anything about her, about what you sentenced her to that night you refused to help."

The familiar anger and helpless fear rolled through Chris's blood. His fists clenched against the hunger for retribution. It would be so easy to inflict a tiny slice of the pain his mother had experienced. The pull of vengeance was almost hypnotic. But the man before him wouldn't pay the price; Chris would. Dr. Desire would. And it wouldn't bring his mother back.

Taking a deliberate step back, Chris put enough space between them to make physical contact impossible.

"Let me give you some advice. Go back to whatever dim-witted divorcée you were conning this time, get down on your hands and knees and beg her for forgiveness. You have a better chance with her than you do with me." Chris smiled, his muscles no longer numb, each and every one aching in protest. He kept the facade anyway.

"Aren't we all high-and-mighty, Dr. Desire. You're no better than I am."

"The hell I'm not."

"We both make our living off seducing women. The only difference is they pay me direct. You have that nice corporation cutting you the check. The end result's the same, boy." He smiled a perfect smile that sent ripples of unease across Chris's body. "Sex sells."

Chris stared, speechless. His brain swirled on the words, but he couldn't form a coherent response.

"I'll let you think about that awhile. See you around."

His father was halfway down the block before Chris had his mouth open and a logical argument ready. Too late. People streamed from the club he'd just left as his father passed by the front door. Yelling at the man now would draw attention he'd rather not have.

Out of the crowd Michael appeared, grabbed his elbow and steered him across the street to his waiting Porsche.

"Who was that you were talking to?"

"No one important."

It wasn't true. He was nothing like his father.

DARRELL SAT IN HIS CAR and fought down the rage. The candy-apple-red Jag was about the only thing of value he owned, and he only owned that because he'd sweet-talked Virginia into putting the title in his name. It was amazing what women would do if you gave them a mind-blowing orgasm.

Selling the car wasn't an option, he wasn't ready to part with it just yet. It was sleek and red and young, and it reminded him of the youth he'd squandered bowing and scraping to women in order to get by.

He'd deserved so much more.

There was another way back to the lifestyle he'd grown accustomed to, the lifestyle he deserved. But it required start-up capital, something he didn't have. But his son did.

Taking a deep breath, he unclenched his hands and laid

them over the leather-wrapped steering wheel. He stroked the soft curve up and down. The feel of it always reminded him of a woman's skin, that smooth, silky place just on the underside of a ripe breast.

It wasn't just the money he missed. His sexual appetites were huge, which was why having only one woman never satisfied him. Or rather *had* never satisfied him. Just one more item on the list of things old age had taken…right along with his looks, his boyish charm, his charisma—everything he needed to function in the high society world of wealthy divorcées.

Damn it! He needed that money and he needed it fast.

Down the street he watched his son speed away in a sports car that strikingly resembled the one he sat in. A small smirk tugged at his lips. They *were* the same.

He wasn't ready to give up just yet. He hadn't spent almost forty years of his life manipulating people into giving him whatever he wanted for nothing. He'd find an in with his son.

Or a weakness he could exploit.

His parting shot had certainly hit home. Darrell hadn't missed the disbelief and utter denial that had skated across Chris's face. So the boy didn't like the idea that he was the apple to his tree.

Well, it was certainly a start.

Maybe tomorrow he'd pay a visit to his famous son's place of employment and see what he could shake out of those branches.

WHY HAD SHE AGREED to this?

Karyn's foot tapped up and down against the polished hardwood floor beneath the table as she waited for Dr. Desire to show up. Her heel clicked in a rhythm that, coming from anyone else, would have annoyed the hell out of her.

She couldn't stop.

At least there wasn't anyone to bother. She sat alone in the quiet room he had reserved for them. Her eyes swept across the cozy space. The dim lighting, flickering candles and mood music all set her nerves on edge. Apparently Dr. Desire hadn't told the restaurant this wasn't a real date.

Karyn tried desperately not to fidget. Or admit that a part of her really wished it were a date. A mixture of anxiety and anticipation churned at the bottom of her stomach. She had no idea what to expect, from Dr. Desire or herself.

"Karyn."

His voice reached her first as he entered the room, melting down her spine in that familiar trail, turning her bones to liquid mush.

He was tall and broad and his presence shrank the already-intimate space. The sheer force of him seemed to consume the excess oxygen in the room, to condense the surroundings to nothing more than a block of space too tiny for them both to occupy—without her brain going fuzzy and her skin flushing hot.

Those billboards did not do him justice.

Karyn knew she was staring, but couldn't help it. Her first real life glimpse of Dr. Desire had her tongue seemingly glued to the roof of her mouth.

His lips curved into a crooked, charming grin, the same one she'd driven past almost every day for the past eighteen months. Candlelight reflected in his blue-gray eyes, catching the smallest glint of mischief lurking there. Maybe it was the flickering light, but she really thought they were more captivating in person.

He stopped by the table, towering over her.

She looked up and up into his sexy face and had to swallow hard to wet her suddenly dry mouth. Her foot kicked into double time beneath the tablecloth. Heat burst through her body and her nipples tingled in a primitive response she hadn't experienced in longer than she could remember.

He packed one hell of a punch.

"Karyn?"

She shook off the daze, cringing at the impression she must be making. By nothing more than walking up beside her, Chris had started a chain reaction inside, awakening places on her body she'd thought long dead.

She stared up into his intense eyes and wanted to cry in frustration. Sure she'd made her share of stupid mistakes in life, but what had she done to deserve this cruel twist of fate? The one man who'd finally revved her engine and he'd already said no. Not just no, *hell,* no, wouldn't touch her with a ten-foot-pole no.

"You're not Karyn? I'm sorry. They told me…"

She still had to get through dinner, preferably without embarrassing herself more than she already had. "Yes. I am… Chris." Standing, she tried hard not to bite her lower lip, a bad habit that tended to surface when she was overwhelmed, and motioned to the chair opposite her. Hopefully the table hid the humming energy that made her knees tremble. At least her foot had stopped tapping.

"I'm sorry I'm late. Business." With his head cocked to the side, he offered a lopsided grin equal parts charm and remorse.

His heat reached out and touched her, mixing with the visceral response still bursting inside. Her entire body warmed, and moisture gathered beneath the unruly mass of hair she'd pulled tight at the nape of her neck.

His eyes snagged her own across the intimate space of their little table, making her feel…caught. Not like a butterfly with its wings pinned down for display. No. The sensation was more like the pull of gravity right before a plane took off. Like some force of nature was holding her back, gathering strength before letting go so she could fly.

She blinked, thinking herself completely insane. She tried to look away but found her gaze drawn back to the magnetic energy he radiated with seemingly little effort.

A shiver of awareness slid down her spine at the intensity of his study. His eyes roamed every inch of her face. Usually that kind of masculine stare would have set her nerves on edge. She was on edge all right. But it had nothing to do with nerves.

Reaching for her water glass, Karyn gulped a swallow, needing busywork for her hands and mind.

He must have taken her silence and hasty chug of water as signs of fear.

Laying his palms flat on the table in front of him, he said, "I want you to know you have nothing to worry about. No expectations. No pressure. We'll have a nice dinner. That's all."

She realized his words and the look of studied sincerity were meant to put her at ease. And if she'd had her normal reaction to a man sitting intimately across from her, they might have been necessary. But Chris Faulkner would not hurt her. She knew this to the soles of her feet.

Fear. Anxiety. Calculating the risks. She thought of none of these normal things. It was the image of those tanned, large, roughened hands on *her* instead of on the snowy tablecloth that had blood whooshing in her ears.

And that surprised her. Yes, in the safety of her mind she had admitted she had a physical response to Chris, to his voice, to the sky-high images that seemed to pepper the city. What red-blooded woman wouldn't? He was gorgeous and had the sort of lazy, husky bedroom voice that drove women crazy.

What she hadn't anticipated was for those rumblings to be exponentially amplified by his actual presence. The reaction she'd had to his picture was safe. She'd never figured on having the opportunity to meet him in person. Now, all she could hear was Anne's voice in the back of her head repeating over and over, "That man knows his way around a woman's body. With him, fear wouldn't be an option. He'd have you naked and panting before you could blink."

She wasn't naked, but the room had definitely become stuffy. She went to tug at her collar only to realize she wasn't wearing her normal high-necked blouse but a low-cut, gauzy silk confection that rubbed deliciously against her skin.

"Karyn?"

His hesitation and low-pitched sound of concern pulled her focus up. Slowly she took in his charcoal-gray suit and white dress shirt, open at his strong throat. Sophisticated and urbane, there was no mistaking him for any man other than Dr. Desire.

She looked up into his dark-blue eyes, at the swirls of gray and flecks of the palest green, and knew this man had it all together. The core of her body clenched.

A smile, one she hadn't seen slip since he'd walked in the door, tipped the corners of those breath-stealing eyes heavenward. Intelligence, laughter, reassurance. Anne was the only other person who'd given her this immediate sense of ease—if you discounted the hum of energy jingling her spine right now.

"Yes." The word came out breathy, almost lost in the muted restaurant sounds from outside the room.

"Are you okay?"

No. She wasn't. For the first time in five years, her body had flooded with heat. A heat she remembered, one she'd feared never feeling again. One she wanted to embrace, explore, capture.

"Yes. I'm…" surprised, excited, achy "…fine."

"Why don't we order some champagne? It'll help settle your nerves."

What nerves? Any nerves she'd felt had melted away the moment he'd walked through the door.

CHRIS WATCHED Karyn from across the table.

She wasn't what he'd expected. When he'd pictured her in his mind she hadn't been ugly—but she hadn't been beautiful, either. Plain, average, unexciting. That's what he'd expected.

What he'd gotten was nothing close to unexciting.

She *was* understated. But she was also…pretty. Fragile. Surprising.

Wisps of auburn hair, dark with only a hint of red, fluttered against her cheeks. A long, shining column spilled over one shoulder, a burst of color against her pale-green shirt. But it was her face that held his attention. Thin, her cheekbones high and sharp, her pale skin seemed to glow luminously in the candlelight.

He'd seen his share of beautiful women in candlelight. Karyn would never be classified as beautiful. She was something more…unique.

Her deep brown eyes flashed with golden glints he could see from half a table away. They were direct, and despite what he'd expected, calm. He fought the urge to breathe in her scent, to let it linger in his senses.

That would not be smart. The beginning tingle of attraction was already racing to the base of his spine. His body tightened. They were familiar signs, ones he'd recognized since he was fourteen and had his first sexual encounter with the older girl next door.

The fact that Karyn was the first woman to rev his engine in months meant nothing. Well, nothing other than the fact that it had been too long since he'd had sex.

It just hadn't been satisfying lately. Oh, he and his partner had both enjoyed orgasms—Dr. Desire couldn't provide anything less—but Chris hadn't been able to shake the feeling that there was something missing. He was tired of playing a role, second-guessing every touch, taste and word against a list of expectations.

The kicker was they were expectations he'd built up himself.

Dr. Desire was a prison of his own making. Women never seemed interested in spending an evening with Chris, they wanted his alter ego.

Karyn was no different. She'd called in to the show wanting something from Dr. Desire, something he wasn't able to give. Looking across the table at her, he watched the sharp edge of her white teeth crease the flesh of her bottom lip, the first outward sign that she wasn't as calm as she wanted him to believe.

One thing was certain: Karyn was not a candidate to break his dry spell. There were consequences, and he didn't just mean for her. His job, his show, the responsibility he had to his listeners, it was all too important to throw away on a sexual whim.

Despite what his fath—Darrell seemed to think, he had standards. Somehow, over the past few years, Dr. Desire had gotten a reputation. Rumors abounded about his sexual prowess, his conquests. Women he'd never met claimed to have spent time in his bed. He hadn't been a monk by any stretch of the imagination, but honestly, if he'd had sex with half the purported number, he would never have slept.

Mutually satisfying sexual gratification—that part of his reputation was all true. That's what the women he did make love with wanted from him and, frankly, that's all he had wanted from them.

Karyn. Karyn needed much more than that. Time. Patience. Understanding. He didn't think he had any of those things.

Not to mention sleeping with her could kill his career. The last thing he needed was for a sensationalized news story to show up about how he'd taken advantage of a rape victim. His listeners wouldn't appreciate that at all. And at the end of the day, the listeners were all that mattered. If he lost them, he lost the show.

Gwen Adair, a reporter for the local newspaper, had been dogging his every step lately, looking for something to make headlines with. She hadn't taken his gentle decline of a rather obvious sexual offer several months ago very well. And while most of the things she'd printed about him so far had been insignificant, he didn't intend to give her something real.

He might have simply fallen into his role as Dr. Desire, but no self-respecting trailer-trash kid would be stupid enough to throw his golden meal ticket away, especially not for sex.

Even sex that his body told him would be fantastic.

Grappling with his control, Chris thought *charm*, and smiled.

Their waiter approached the table and took his champagne order. Leaning over, the man also poured more water into Karyn's glass. It hadn't been anywhere close to empty; in fact, it looked like she'd taken maybe two sips. She glanced up, smiling slightly at the other man with those big, brown eyes.

A seed of something he couldn't quite name lodged somewhere in his chest. His eyes narrowed as he watched the two interact.

He didn't appreciate the other man's blatant interest in his date. Or the way he crowded into Karyn's space. But as Chris's attention swung back to her, the seed dissolved. He couldn't miss the way she slid back into her chair.

She chuckled at some inane comment, and understanding dawned. She was trying to project the image of a carefree woman. But Chris heard the strain in the delicate noise, and her wildly tapping foot beneath the table didn't escape his notice, either. It brushed against his pant leg with each upswing.

As the man slid away to fill their request, Chris watched her chest rise and fall on a silent sigh of relief.

"Why didn't you just tell him to leave you alone?"

"What?" She glanced up, her wide brown eyes looking directly at him, into him.

His breath caught and held while he studied her. Determination, acceptance and a tiny spark of fear clouded her gaze. But as he watched, the golden specks caught fire and flashed with something completely primitive and completely feminine.

Something deep inside him responded. His heart sped up and the blood quickened, rushing downward. He leaned forward, wanting to be sure it hadn't been a trick of the light, but as he did she blinked and it was gone.

"Why didn't you tell him to back off? You were obviously uncomfortable with him standing so close."

She looked away for a moment before answering. "Because it isn't his problem. He didn't do anything wrong."

"But neither did you."

Her lips ghosted up in the faint beginnings of a smile before flatlining again.

He would have said more, but the man returned with their bottle at that moment. Through the uncorking ritual, Chris watched her.

Her delicate fingers grasped the stem of her glass flute, settling the rim between her lush lips, the bottom one slightly fuller than the top. Her disproportioned mouth was the one anomaly to her appearance. One he liked. Something that made her unique and delightfully imperfect. Her pale throat worked over a mouthful of the bubbling wine as her eyes scanned the oversize menu before her.

How this woman had gotten through the past five years without touching a man, let alone sleeping with one, he couldn't figure out.

"I hope you're not nervous or embarrassed."

She laughed, the last thing he'd expected. But the sound rolled through him, reverberating inside his chest like the pounding bass in the classic rock he loved to listen to late at night, alone in the dark after his show.

"So it's pretty common for your dates to proposition you before dinner even begins? That's good to know."

Her ability to laugh at herself and their unusual situation impressed him. And her strength astounded him. Unless you knew what signs to look for, you'd never guess that she was anything but relaxed.

"As a matter of fact, I'm pretty used to that." He flashed her a smile meant to bring back that laugh. "But I don't usually agree to dates with those women, so you're a first."

He regretted the words the moment they left his mouth as the spark in her eyes dulled and her cheeks bloomed red. "However, I have been on a ton of first dates and, as you can see, have lived to tell the tales. I promise this won't hurt. You might even find you like me."

"I already like you, Chris."

"You like my public persona. That guy isn't all I am."

Now why had he said that? It didn't matter. She could like whoever she wanted—Dr. Desire, Chris Faulkner, the waiter. After this night it wouldn't make a damn bit of difference. No matter how appealing and beautiful she was, he wasn't getting involved. End of story.

"I'd like to think I'm not that shallow. I realize your job isn't all there is to know about you. But I've learned a lot, more than you probably think, by listening to the advice you give."

"Like what?"

"I know that you have a wickedly sarcastic sense of humor."

Chris rocked back into his chair, dropping the menu he hadn't really been looking at anyway.

"Usually those comments are at the expense of someone's pride, and afterward I feel horrible."

"See, I knew it. Under that tough, man's-man persona there's a softy. You're a nice guy."

"No. A nice guy wouldn't say the stuff in the first place. Or wouldn't continue saying it. I said I feel guilty, but only for a second."

"Well, that's because the person on the other end usually needs some sense knocked into them."

Maybe she did understand him. He'd often thought he'd carefully compartmentalized his true persona from the polished, charming Dr. Desire, the voice and personality that garnered ratings and multiyear contracts. Maybe not.

"That's one reason I called the show. Not because you were soft and nice. But because you're hard and tough and usually right. I trust you to tell me what I need to hear."

"What do you need to hear?" His voice dipped lower than he'd intended. He hoped she hadn't noticed. The last thing he wanted to do was make her uncomfortable.

She waved her hands between them. "This is not supposed to be a pop psych session. Just dinner."

She was right. He'd walked into the restaurant intent on proving to Karyn she could enjoy a nice dinner out with a man, a stranger, without having to deal with the complicated issues. He'd specifically set out *not* to turn on Dr. Desire. He wanted to stay as far away as possible from that proposition she claimed had *just* slipped out. He didn't want to give her another chance to mention what she needed from him, how he could help solve all her sexual problems.

He couldn't solve anything. At the moment, however, his libido was sorely tempted to try.

4

ALL THROUGH DINNER Karyn felt as if she was walking a tight-rope. Despite the fact that every cell in her body seemed swollen, excited, expectant, somehow she managed to keep her reaction to herself. Or she hoped she had.

Leaning toward him across the table was normal, right? She wanted to hear him over the kitchen clatter coming from behind the doors. And so what that she'd forgotten and let their hands touch. Accident. Pure accident. She just hoped Chris hadn't noticed that when dessert arrived and her tongue darted across her lips in anticipation, she hadn't been staring at his chocolate tart.

"You should try this. It's wonderful." Chris looked at her across the table, his fork halfway to his almost-empty plate, a thoroughly satisfied smile on his face. Chocolate could do that to a person.

She started to protest, opening her mouth to insist she was full already. But he didn't give her a chance. Chris reached across the table, putting his fork loaded down with rich creamy mousse and a buttery, flaky crust into her mouth. Her lips closed around the cold metal in reflex. The sinful treat melted on her tongue.

Their eyes collided. Electricity snapped from his hand to her lips through the conduit of the fork. He jerked back, pulling it through her still-pursed lips. It stayed suspended between them, wavering slightly from the force of his hold.

She swallowed, not tasting the rich pastry anymore, but what she imagined his kiss would be like, spicy with a hint of sweet temptation.

He cleared his throat, the sound seeming to break their connection. "I'm sorry."

"No. It was wonderful."

Karyn dropped her eyes to the tablecloth before her, trying to regain her focus.

This is not a date.

She let the words swirl around in her brain. Maybe this time she'd remember them.

Life was so unfair. The first man she'd been attracted to—and if that wasn't the understatement of the century, she didn't know what was—in five long, lonely years, and she'd had to blow it by propositioning him on the radio. She was going to kill Anne.

Thankfully their waiter broke the tension. "Would you like anything else? More wine? Coffee?"

Karyn looked to Chris. It was a natural gesture, something she hadn't experienced in too long. Looking to someone else, a man, for his opinion before making a decision. It wasn't that she couldn't do it on her own, it was just…nice.

With a raised brow, he asked a silent question. The intimate gesture tightened her chest. She ignored the twinge of longing that went with it and gave a negative shake of her head.

Breaking the connection, he responded, "No thank you," paid their bill, held her chair and led her through the crowded restaurant to the front door.

He didn't touch her, like he probably would have with a real date, and she didn't know whether to be grateful or upset.

He'd been very considerate, making sure nothing he did or said might upset her. And really, she appreciated it. But God, she wanted his hands on her. At the small of her back guiding her out. Wrapped around her shoulders, tucking her in tight to his body. Running over her naked, heated skin.

She dragged a breath in through clamped teeth, letting the tiny whistle distract her. Why him? Why now? Why the one man she couldn't have?

Before the double doors leading outside, he stopped and pulled her from the flow of traffic.

"I enjoyed this. And you didn't seem to be too uncomfortable."

"No. I had a good time. I really appreciate your help." She smiled, hoping none of the sexual attraction suffusing every pore shone through her face.

"Sure." Chris's gaze jumped around, his smile a little strained.

Feeling awkward herself, because for some strange reason she really didn't want their night to end, she took a halting step away from him.

"Well…thanks."

Was it her imagination or had he taken a step toward her?

"I hope everything works out. If you still need information on therapists, call my producer, Michael."

Therapists. She didn't want to talk about therapists with him. She wanted to kiss him senseless. Or rather, she wanted him to kiss *her* senseless. But she nodded anyway, ignoring the feeling fizzing in her veins, and turned to go.

Pushing through the tiny lobby out into the hot, muggy August night, Karyn sensed Chris following behind her. The heat off his body rivaled the heat still curling up from the sidewalk an hour after dusk. Her hands fisted around the straps of her brown, all-purpose purse. In a bid for distraction, she began rustling inside for the keys to her car. She lifted up old receipts, her stuffed wallet, cell phone, but couldn't find her keys. They were in there somewhere; she distinctly remembered throwing them into her own personal black hole before she'd walked in the door.

"Problem?"

"No. I can't find my keys, but they're in here somewhere." She hoped he'd go on ahead.

Walking and rummaging at the same time, she drew up short when Chris's hand locked around her elbow. Looking up in surprise, she stopped at the sight before her. Her breath backed into her lungs and the panic she'd expected all night rushed in. Her hands shook, almost dropping the messy jumble of her life onto the pavement at her feet.

Chris reached around and plucked the dangling leather from her numb fingers before the disaster could get any worse.

A half-dozen people, with flashing cameras, digital voice recorders and notebooks in hand, stood before her. So intent on finding her keys, she'd crossed the parking lot completely oblivious to the tiny cluster around the cars.

"Dr. Desire, introduce us to your date."

"Who's your latest conquest?"

"Is it Katy?"

"Are you going to sleep with her?"

The words flew, making her head spin and startling her out of the jaw-dropping stupor she'd been shocked into.

But before she could do or say anything—probably something she'd regret—Chris took over.

"Now, guys, I'm sure you can understand why I don't want my dates being accosted. Pretty soon no one will want to go out with me. And that would not help my reputation at all."

Chris's laugh rolled over the crowd, the men and women joining in. He flung an arm across her shoulders, the muscles beneath his embrace pulling tight.

Sure, now he touched her.

"So is this Katy, your little rape victim?" A husky voice from the back rose above the noise.

Her heart sped up, pounding in her ears so loud it muffled all other sounds.

A classic brunette detached herself from the back of the group, splitting them like the red sea and floating up to Chris on heels so high Karyn didn't know how the woman walked without breaking her ankle. She stopped before him, close enough that if she breathed hard her breasts would rub against his chest.

"No, Gwen, this is Karyn."

Ice-blue eyes flicked to Karyn, traveling up and down. They missed nothing. She fought the urge to reach up and smooth the stray strands of hair that insisted on blowing in the stingy summer breeze. Ms. High-and-Mighty certainly didn't have a hair out of place. And Karyn would bet the woman didn't sweat, either. Her glands wouldn't think of rebelling.

Apparently even more confident after what she'd seen, the woman turned her attention to Chris, moving even closer—though Karyn didn't see how she could have accomplished that without defying the laws of physics.

"You've heard the calls, Chris. The public wants to know this woman's story. Don't forget, you serve the public, too."

"Wrong, Gwen. I serve my listeners. My job is to help them and no matter what you—" Chris looked out into the crowd, his dark eyes going flinty "—or the rest of you think, exposing Katy to public scrutiny wouldn't serve any purpose other than to embarrass and hurt her. I'm certain if she wanted to share more of her story, you'd be the first ones she'd call."

"No." Gwen's cold eyes met Karyn's. "She called you."

Ignoring that parting shot, Chris let his gaze sweep across the crowd. His lips curled into a smile that just an hour ago she would have believed, and said, "Good night."

Keeping his arm around her, Chris steered her away from the crowd. But instead of heading toward her car, parked four rows away, he stopped at a flashy sports car several feet from the watching press.

Opening the red door, he placed her into the passenger seat before rounding the car and slipping in the driver's side.

He put the key in the ignition, but didn't crank the car. He simply sat for a moment, staring ahead.

"I'm sorry about that."

"How the hell did they know where we'd be?"

"I have no idea." His hands flexed around the steering wheel, his knuckles going white. "But my guess is some intern or assistant thought they'd make a quick buck."

He turned in his seat, draping an arm over the steering wheel to face her. "I'm really sorry. I only told a couple key people at the station. Somehow it went further."

She grabbed on to the anger flowing through her, using it to combat the terror she expected to hit at any moment. Sitting in this car, so close and confined with Chris should make her quake inside.

She was disoriented and surprised when it didn't.

She'd been raped in the backseat of a tiny sedan. It wasn't a sports car, but more like a molded metal box on wheels, amounting to the same thing.

Not only wasn't she panicking, but she actually turned to face him. She wasn't thinking about how close he was so she could calculate an escape. No, her mind whirred, plotting how she could get closer.

Her anger melted away, replaced by another emotion, equally hot and passionate. She pushed it back. He'd already turned her down once. She wasn't about to subject herself to another round of humiliation.

"Look, it doesn't matter. I appreciate you lying to them, but I could have handled myself. I might be a little damaged but I'm not helpless."

"I didn't say you were."

"Maybe not, but you certainly implied it with that knight-in-shining-armor routine back there."

"You said you didn't want publicity. So I took care of it."

"Look, I've had experience handling the media. I'm a big girl and can swim just fine with the sharks. But I prefer not to."

His gaze sharpened. "All right. Next time I'll go ahead and tell them who you are. Would that be better?"

The temperature inside the car inched up. Karyn realized their argument wasn't entirely responsible for the shift in atmosphere.

Twisting so she could peer out the tiny back window, she registered the circling vultures still waiting. A couple of flashes popped in the ever darkening night.

"Whatever. Thanks for dinner. I appreciate your effort. Have a nice life." She moved to open the door, but before she could, Chris reached out a hand to stop her.

"You can't leave."

"The hell I can't."

"No. How will it look?" Chris nodded his head sideways, toward the back window and the tiny cluster of people standing behind them.

Damn! He was right. If they left in separate cars, they'd know immediately that she wasn't just some date he'd taken out on a Saturday night. And they'd see her license plate number.

Turning back to face him, she glared. "Great. So what do you suggest?"

"Ever been to Hickman's Point?"

Hickman's Point? "No. And we're not going."

Any other time, Karyn might have thought she'd died and gone to heaven. The sexiest, most charismatic, most amazing man she'd ever met was asking her to go parking. But not because he actually wanted to kiss and touch her.

If he had, she'd have said yes in a heartbeat.

No. She'd been the one fantasizing about all the fun they could have in the compact sports car. He wouldn't even understand how significant that fact was to her. She hadn't fantasized about anything besides winning the lottery or landing a promotion in five years.

And here he was, sex on a platter, and all she could think about was licking him clean—and he just wanted to throw the press off their trail. It was enough to make a girl cry.

When they pulled up to her apartment several minutes later, she didn't question how he'd known her address. He'd found her phone number and her real name. Getting out, she headed for her front door, leaving him and her chance for an ordinary life behind. This man had shown her a glimpse of normalcy. Somehow she didn't think that would readily happen again.

"I'm really sorry about the way this turned out, about the reporters."

His voice floated to her on the late-night breeze. The hot August night had cooled a little, not enough to need to cover her bare arms, but enough that the gentle wind felt refreshing on her skin. And if she hoped for a moment his hands would brush across it instead, she pushed that thought out of her mind.

"It's not your fault."

"But it is. I'll find out what happened, who leaked the information."

Stopping at the door to her ground-floor apartment, she turned around to face him.

"It doesn't matter, Chris. No harm done. Please, just forget about it."

"Let me get your car at least."

"I'll take care of it tomorrow." With sudden conviction, she decided it wouldn't matter if her Honda sat in the parking lot all night. Tomorrow was Sunday. She'd deal with it later.

"I'll take care of it. Please. Give me the keys."

"No, really—"

"Give me the keys, Karyn."

That firm, dark voice skittered across her spine, sending a wave of awareness with it. Another shot of adrenaline pushed through her veins and suddenly she didn't seem as drained as she had a moment ago. Before she realized what she was doing, she'd reached into her bag, pulled out her pile of keys and dropped them into his waiting palm.

"Which one's your house key?"

She pointed mutely at one of them.

He stepped up to the door, and she found herself pushed into the corner, trapped by the edge of her porch and the solid wall of man before her.

Despite the gentle evening breeze, her skin felt hot and tight.

He took the key, ignoring her completely, inserted it into the lock and twisted. She heard the rasp of metal against metal, the loud pop as the lock released. But all that only registered in some back corner of her mind.

Her senses were filled with Chris. The gentle sound of his breathing. The warm, musky scent of his spicy cologne. The underlying smell of confident, sexy male. The scent swirled in her mouth, running over her tongue and taste buds until she had to resist the urge to dart it out for a fuller taste.

Her eyes traveled from the tailored suit jacket he wore to the cotton dress shirt underneath, the bunch and play of muscles beneath the fabric as his hands worked at her door. The flex and pull called to her like a snake charmer, mesmerizing her to touch.

Touch. The one thing she hadn't done. The one sense that hadn't been filled with him all night. A brief brush of fingers wouldn't be enough. She wanted to run her hands over the muscles and lose herself in the press of him beneath her.

She hadn't felt this way in years. This driving need to take, to fulfill her basic purpose for existing. She was so worried it was a fleeting experience, one that would disappear with him.

She couldn't stop the motion. Her hand lifted. Her palm pushed through the heavy night air. And as he turned to her, holding open the door, she reached for him.

She heard his sudden intake of breath as her palm connected with his chest.

Heat. It was the first thing that registered. The heat from his skin seeped through the tightly woven strands of cotton to radiate up her arm and leave her slightly breathless, like when she'd fallen out of her tree house as a little girl.

The valleys and planes beneath registered next, filling the curve of her palm before dropping away. The need to explore pounded in her temples, through her blood. And so she did, letting her hand shift over him, up to touch the swirling dark hair that peeked out at his open collar and down over the ripples of muscles marching across his abs to the waistband of his slacks, her fingers playing dangerously at the edge.

Reality flashed into focus with the same glaring intrusion as the photographers from an hour before. What was she doing?

Karyn would have taken a step away, for herself and to show him something had changed, but the wall at her back prevented her from doing so.

Her gaze stayed glued to his chest. Her cheeks flamed with embarrassment, but she couldn't seem to drag her gaze up to look into his eyes. She wasn't sure what she'd find there, but something told her it would be nothing she wanted to see.

His chest rose with even breaths. One, two, three in. One, two, three out. She counted and waited, holding her own breath, not sure what she wanted next.

Chris reached out, put a finger beneath her chin and tipped her head up until her eyes caught his.

They were dark and deep and swirling with something she didn't feel the need to dwell on.

They stood, staring at each other for a moment. She had no idea what he was seeing in her, her emotions were so jumbled up inside even she wasn't entirely sure what she was feeling, what would show through.

He was going to kiss her. She saw the spark of decision in his eyes, the slight lean of his body as he moved toward her.

"Thank you for a wonderful evening, Karyn."

Her mind flashed to one of his shows, one where he'd admonished a caller for upsetting his date by not remembering her name. "Guys, if you can't remember her name make something up, darling, honey, sweetheart. Chances are you won't be calling her back if you already can't remember who to ask for in the morning. But don't ruin her evening just because you're a prick."

Well, at least he'd remembered her name. As he moved forward, she braced herself for the coming kiss. She wasn't entirely sure what her reaction would be, but she wanted to know the feel of his mouth against her own. Wanted Chris to be the first man to touch her in that intimate way since that long-ago night. Her lips parted in anticipation, and her eyelids fluttered shut.

Her last thought as the gap between them closed was whether or not the fact that he remembered her name meant he'd be calling in the morning.

Right before his lips brushed across her…forehead.

SON OF A BITCH! What the hell was he doing?

Chris walked down the sidewalk toward his car, cringing at the loud echo of Karyn's door closing behind him.

He wanted to turn around, yank open that door and kiss the fire out of them both. But he wouldn't.

Damn. All he'd done was touch her forehead and his cock

was hard enough to chisel rock. The mere thought of his hands running over her naked skin aroused him faster and more strongly than actually touching a woman had in months.

Slipping behind the wheel of his Porsche, he fought the throbbing urge to get right back out. Sex with Karyn wasn't a possibility. She might think he could solve her sexual issues, but he couldn't.

He'd seen the expectant look in her eyes, the way her lids had fluttered closed with complete abandon and trust. She shouldn't trust him. He couldn't save her.

And even if he wanted to try, doing so had the potential to topple the persona he'd built his life around. And once the facade was gone so was his livelihood, his safety net.

Wild energy buzzed through his blood. Maybe he could channel it with speed. He certainly couldn't bleed it off the way his body urged.

It had to be some cruel twist of fate. The only woman he'd wanted in months and he couldn't have her. Couldn't with a capital *C*.

Dr. Desire wouldn't have this dilemma. He'd instinctively know the way to get what he wanted without jeopardizing anything important.

Chris on the other hand… He knew there were inescapable ramifications. His show was the only thing separating him from the tenuous existence of his childhood and painful feelings of powerlessness and inadequacy that he never wanted to experience again.

The image of his father popped into his brain. A grown, weathered man well past his prime—who looked too much like him for comfort—standing with his hand out, begging for money.

Chris would not let his life dissolve back into that, into depending on anyone but himself for survival.

He had a decent life. He'd worked hard for what he had. No

matter how much he wanted to lose himself in Karyn's untapped heat, it wasn't worth the risk.

His raging hard-on didn't agree with him at the moment, but he'd ignore it until it did.

He couldn't sleep with her.

What he could do was find out who had leaked the information about their dinner. And when he did…someone would pay.

5

_____

"WHAT THE HELL is going on?"

Karyn jerked, stabbing herself with her pen and sending black ink gliding across the back of her hand. She blinked at Anne, disoriented and a little unsteady.

"What are you talking about?"

"This," her friend replied, slapping a folded newspaper on top of the fifty-page, minuscule print, year-to-date expense report she'd been reading before Anne's incredulous voice had interrupted.

Karyn stared; she'd never seen Anne so agitated. Leaning forward, she furiously scanned the page.

"There's a gala at Ashcroft on Saturday?" Karyn looked up. "You want an invitation? You're the one with family in high places."

"No. Not that." Anne glared and pointed to the bottom of the page. "This. The story about Dr. Desire. Accompanied by a picture of him with you."

"What?" Snatching the flimsy paper from her desk, Karyn stared at the unmistakable picture of Chris…with his arm draped around her shoulders.

It had been three days since their "date," long enough for her to hope that the photographers who'd been outside that night had decided she was too boring to mention. Apparently not.

Scanning the short paragraphs beside the photo, Karyn

realized she was boring. It was Chris they were interested in. There was a brief line of speculation about who she was, but most of the story focused on bashing Chris's reputation. After reading the byline—Gwen Adair—a few things fell into place. She'd thought there had been some nasty undercurrents between the brunette and Chris the other night. She'd simply been too preoccupied to care.

Karyn took in the image, the way Chris leaned toward her, their bodies touching from shoulder to hip. The smiling intensity in his eyes. The seemingly happy couple.

A mixture of emotions bubbled up inside.

On the forehead. God. Every time she thought of it she vacillated between a desire to smack the man senseless or kiss them both sane.

How could he? There she'd been, about to take a giant step, one she'd been dreading for the past several years. And when she was finally ready, he'd kissed her on the forehead. The forehead.

Something pricked the center of her palm. Karyn looked down to find the newspaper crumpled in her fist.

Ever since that night, he'd visited her in her dreams, leaving her hot and needy in the morning. Looking down at the crumpled image of him, she couldn't stop the slow roll her tummy took.

"You never said anything. You had a date with Dr. Desire and you didn't tell me?" Anne's voice bounced off the cube's flimsy gray walls.

Karyn shot up from her desk, pulling her friend in and down. "Shush."

"A little late now." Anne snatched the paper from her hand, pointing at the picture. "Everyone already knows." Her eyebrows beetled with concern. "How could you not tell me, Kar? I'm supposed to be your best friend."

Pushing her into the cheaply upholstered chair stuck in the

corner, Karyn whispered, "You are. It wasn't a date…precisely."

Anne cocked an eyebrow. "You look cozy enough in this picture. Besides, that isn't the point. The last thing I knew you were wishing you'd never made that phone call. Now you show up in the paper with Dr. Desire plastered against your body."

"He is not plastered. He was just acting for the reporters, nothing more."

Anne let out a derisive snort. "If he's acting, then he missed his calling. He shouldn't be behind a microphone; he should be in front of a camera."

Karyn leaned forward, closing the space between them. Unease bubbled through her as she glanced once around before whispering, "Look, the station found out who I was. He called and asked me to dinner so they could announce on the show they were getting Katy help. No big deal."

"No big deal." Anne shook her head, the look on her face an upsetting mixture of hurt and disappointment. "God, I should be so mad at you."

"I'm sor—"

"But I can't be." Her friend waved the unfinished apology away and pushed forward with eager anticipation. "Tell me everything."

Karyn let out a sigh of relief. But that didn't mean she was willing to spill her guts. "There isn't—"

"You owe me details, Karyn." She scooted her chair closer so they were face-to-face. "Immediately. Every dirty, sordid one."

Karyn gave her as many as she could, weaving fact and a bit of fiction together so she wouldn't have to admit her lapse of sanity on the front porch.

"Besides, it doesn't matter what happened. I won't be seeing him again."

"How do you know that?" Anne reached for the newspaper and pointed to the picture there. "The man in this picture looks pretty into you."

"Trust me. He didn't even knock when he dropped off my car. He left the keys in the mail slot."

"If you say so." Anne gave her an I-won't-waste-my-breath-arguing smile and left in her usual blur.

Allowing herself one last look at the picture—ignoring the impulse to run a finger over his body—Karyn folded the paper into a neat, tidy square. She was just about to toss it into the trash can beside her desk and get back to work when Anne's voice rang out through the partitioned space.

"Oh my God."

Leaping from her desk, Karyn stuck her head around her wall, certain she was about to see smoke pouring from a cubicle. Instead Anne crouched on the floor, papers scattered at her feet. A man knelt beside her, his back to Karyn, helping her gather the pages.

He made a low, rumbled reply to something Anne said, but Karyn couldn't hear the words. Her friend laughed, looked up into his face and gave her patented model-bright smile.

She shook her head. Anne just had the ability to flatten men, figuratively and literally.

She was about to walk over and rib her friend when the man turned and stopped her dead.

He might have on tight blue jeans and a T-shirt instead of his trademark *GQ* suit, but from the profile there was no mistaking Dr. Desire.

"Oh, hell!"

KARYN'S VOICE CAUGHT Chris's attention and he whipped his head around to find her. She stood, stock-still, half in and half out of a cubicle. Next to the drab gray surroundings, her red-brown hair and dark eyes stood out. Somehow she managed to combine confidence and fragility into the same amazing frame.

But it didn't matter. He was not here to be entranced. He was here to apologize.

He needed to make sure she was okay. At least, that's what he kept telling himself. It had absolutely nothing to do with the sense that he'd left something incomplete, though he'd been battling that unsettling feeling ever since he'd walked away from her front porch.

This was a simple, quick errand.

His eyes traveled the length of her lithe body. She wore a T-shirt of some silky-looking material that clung to her every curve paired with a skirt that left her legs bare. From his vantage point crouched on the floor, he had a perfect view— and few defenses against the sight of her.

He'd convinced himself it had been a figment of his imagination, the all-consuming attraction he'd fought as he'd driven away. Her pull couldn't be that strong. Not on him. He was jaded. He'd seen and heard it all.

But as he looked up into her face, chin cocked, shoulders thrust back, something between anger and desire flooding her eyes, he realized he'd been wrong. His memory hadn't exaggerated the sensation. It hadn't even come close.

He should leave now, before he did something stupid like act on the fantasies inundating his brain. And he would. As soon as he apologized like he'd planned.

"Can I have those back?"

The perky blonde with the perfect curls was looking up at him expectantly.

"Absolutely. Sorry."

Shoving the crumpled mess into her hands, he crossed to Karyn, promptly forgetting everything but her.

"What are you doing here, Chris?"

The sharp, crisp sound in her voice should have given him pause, but the tiny flame flickering in her eyes was enough of a distraction that he didn't let it bother him.

"We need to talk. Do you have a minute?"

She stared. He could see the protest forming, watched her lips pull into a negative pucker. But before she could get it out he found himself with an unlikely ally.

"Sure. She can take a break." The blonde appeared at his elbow, crowding into the tight aisle, a huge smile on her face and a not-so-subtle look in her eye. "You were just going to run down the street for coffee anyway. Right, Karyn?"

He couldn't hide his smile when Karyn scowled.

"Actually, I'm in the middle of this expense report." She turned to him with a falsely apologetic expression. The fact that she wanted nothing to do with him should have stung. Instead it made Chris want to rile her a bit. "Then I need to run the receivables, cash flow.... I've got a major meeting first thing in the morning."

"Your meeting's tomorrow, mine's today. And I need a boost of caffeine before I head into the lion's den." The blonde, clearly Karyn's friend, turned her full attention to him. He had no doubt it was a tactic meant to cut off any protest. A clever one.

"Who knew selling boring mechanical widgets could be such a blood sport? No one mentioned *that* in marketing class. Of course, no one thought I'd actually be using my degree so maybe they didn't think I'd need to know."

He watched Karyn throw a daggered look at her chattering friend and clamped his teeth tight against another smile. He really liked this woman.

Leaning against the cloth-covered wall, he crossed his arms over his chest, and for the first time since he'd walked into the restaurant the other day, he finally felt back on solid ground.

"Surely you're not going to leave your friend high and dry? I'm happy to go with you. Kill two birds with one stone."

Karyn looked from one to the other, clearly unhappy with the turn of events. The blonde cocked an eyebrow and murmured something about opportunity and hiding. Through clenched teeth Karyn said, "Fine. I'll get my purse."

She might not have been happy about it, but at least she was going. He listened to the small sounds coming from inside her cubicle: her desk drawer rolling open and slamming shut. A muffled curse and the telltale jingling of keys.

"Where's my cell?" floated out on a grumble, making him swallow a laugh.

"We might be a few minutes. I'm Anne, Karyn's best friend."

Chris stuck out his hand. "I'm Chris."

"I know who you are." The blonde sidled a bit closer. From anyone else he would have taken the move as a blatant come-on, but not from her. Not paired with the mama-bear-protecting-her-young scowl that crinkled her eyes.

"You better not do anything to hurt her. She's had it rough, but you already know that, don't you?" The smile she flashed had nothing to do with humor.

After having known her for all of five minutes, he'd bet his custom-designed pool table that she rarely showed this fierce side of her personality to anyone. He didn't know whether to laugh over her misguided notion that Karyn needed protection from him, or applaud her for her loyalty.

Fighting the urge to hold up open palms in a gesture of surrender he said, "We're just friends."

"Yeah, right." She shifted away. Somehow the widening gap between them didn't make him feel any more comfortable. "I know lust when I see it. Just remember I've got her back. Karyn might not stoop to revenge, but I have no problem with physical retribution."

The fact that she recognized the attraction he was trying desperately to deny set his nerves on edge. He obviously wasn't doing a very good job.

"Really. We're not involved."

Anne shrugged. "Whatever. Just remember."

Before he could pursue it further, convince them both that he meant what he said, Karyn reappeared. Snagging him by the elbow, she tugged him around and whisked him down the hall.

As they walked through the Art Deco lobby, he had the completely insane urge to whistle. For the first time in days he felt happy. Shit, for the first time in months he felt happy.

But Karyn obviously wasn't. She marched out before him, the double glass doors almost swinging back to slam into him. It didn't take a self-proclaimed expert on women to know she was pissed. He could only assume it was the picture.

The wet August heat slapped him in the face as they stepped out onto the blacktop parking lot. He'd lived in the South all his life, but somehow the breath-stealing heat of the city was completely different from the smoldering earthy summer of home. Of course, Logan's Cross didn't have miles of high-rise buildings to bounce the heat around.

Grabbing Karyn's arm, he slowed her pace and steered her over a couple of rows to his car.

"I think I should drive."

"No. I'll drive."

"Angry driving is dangerous. I'd never forgive myself if something happened." He stared into that expressive, impressive face. She was soft, silent, strong. But underneath that controlled exterior he detected a passion she hadn't tapped, didn't trust and possibly didn't understand.

Fire flared in her deep-brown eyes, triggering an overwhelming urge in him to help her channel that anger, that passion.

Jerking out of his grasp, Karyn turned on him, her back pressed to the passenger door. "What are you doing here?"

"Going for coffee. I thought that's what you wanted."

She narrowed her eyes, her mouth, even her cheeks pulled tight. He could see the storm flashing behind those deep brown pools, knew she wanted to unleash several choice words. But she wouldn't. The insides of her cheeks were going to hurt from biting those words back. He would advise her to just let go.

Through clenched teeth she said, "Why did you come to see me?"

He had no idea. Oh, when he'd left the office he'd known why he was driving halfway across town. But now he wasn't so positive. Now, standing a foot from her, the tempting scent of something fruity, seductive and female was clouding his brain, his focus, his purpose. He wanted nothing more than to close that gap, to lean into this woman and take what he hadn't the other night.

Shaking the thought from his head, he tried to concentrate on something other than her.

"I wanted to make sure you were all right and to tell you it was an employee of the restaurant who tipped off the press. He won't be doing that again."

"You wanted to make sure I wasn't pissed about the picture."

"Well, if we're being honest, yes."

The last thing he expected was to hear her laugh. And while the rolling cadence echoed somewhere close to his abdomen, there was something disturbingly wrong with the sound.

"I don't see how that's funny," he said.

She sucked in a deep breath. He was close enough to hear the reverberation, to see the heavy rise and fall of her chest. A flash of how that movement would feel against his naked skin almost stole his breath.

Damn, what was wrong with him?

"At least you're honest. Ulterior motives. That makes sense after the other night."

"What do you mean?"

"Let's just say after the way our night ended I only expected to see you on park benches and passing buses."

Now he was really confused.

"How it ended? What are you talking about?"

"Nothing. Forget it. It's not important anymore. Are we going for coffee or not?"

Crap. If there was one unequivocal thing he knew about women it was that the word *nothing* was a lie. But he honestly had no idea what the true problem was.

"Obviously it is important to you. Are you upset that I didn't call? Because we agreed the other night was a one-time deal." Although, he'd found himself picking up the phone several times over the last few days, usually after thinking about that night and her porch.

Of course he'd quickly slammed it back down. This woman had way too much baggage, a hell of a lot more than he could handle. She needed something from him he simply wasn't qualified or prepared to give.

She shifted, her swaying hips snatching his attention. Blood rushed from his head straight to his cock. He took a half step back in an effort to relieve the pressure.

Why? Why was she the only woman in months to bring on this sudden, intense reaction? He talked about sex every day. Women threw themselves at him all the time. So why was the one off-limits woman, a woman more damaged than he was, the only one to make him want this way?

"Oh, I understand. I understand completely. If being constantly reminded that our date wasn't real hadn't been enough, having you kiss my forehead certainly was."

Her teeth were clenched so tightly, he could practically hear the enamel cracking from the pressure. Her eyes glowed with emotion, those shots of gold pulsing, pulling him in.

He fought against the attraction. Even in anger she looked fragile. He'd promised himself, everyone at the station, but most importantly Karyn, that he wouldn't touch her. And he wouldn't. Because while his body thought doing so might just be the best damn thing in this world, his mind said it might just be the worst mistake he'd ever make—and he'd made plenty.

It had been a battle between his integrity and desire, but when he'd walked away the other night, knowing she'd had a mostly pleasant evening, he'd felt the sacrifice well worth the effort. He'd done as much as he could to help her.

Yes, he'd known she'd wanted a kiss in the shadows of her dark porch. He'd have been an idiot not to. He hadn't fulfilled that desire, not only because he'd known how wrong touching her would be for both of them, but because he'd wanted that kiss more than his next breath. He'd denied himself and whether she realized it or not had probably saved her from a bad situation.

Looking at the woman—shoulders thrust back, emotion pinking her cheeks, and that damned determined stare—he wasn't certain he could manage to deny himself again. Her pull was just too strong, and he'd gone without a woman in his bed for so long. He tried to ignore the taunting voice in his head that told him no one else had been worth the risk, to his career or to his sanity.

"Look, I did you a favor. You were in the moment. Later, you would have regretted the impulse." They both would have.

"I've waited five years. Do you have any idea how frustrating it is to want sex, to crave the touch of another human being, but to not be able to have it? Trust me, regret wouldn't have come close."

His stomach caved and his penis swelled tight against the fly of his jeans. He had *some* idea.

He took a step toward her, unable to stop. "Trust *me,* sex with the wrong person isn't that fulfilling. That isn't what you need."

"How do you know what I need?" Her words lost their biting edge, instead turning soft and liquid along with her eyes.

"Dr. Desire, remember?"

Her tongue sneaked out, darting over that swollen bottom lip. "You don't have all the answers."

Her voice echoed through his brain. He might not know how to solve her problem, but he certainly had the personal sexual experience to back up the advice he gave on his show. He knew women, knew how they thought and what they wanted. And if her words fisted in his chest, wrapping around the one kernel of doubt he kept hidden from everyone else…he'd simply ignore it.

The sexual awareness pulsing through him wasn't so easy to dismiss.

"A kiss? Is that what this is about?" Chris took another, deliberate step forward, framing her with his body. He could show her a few of the answers he did have. "Far be it from me to deny a woman."

Even as the barest shift of body brought him flush against her, his brain screamed, *Bad idea.*

Acceptance and anticipation chased through her eyes. He paused the barest moment, giving her one last chance to protest before moving in to take what he wanted. Once their mouths touched it would be too late.

Her fingers curled into fists at her side. Her eyes blazed, but she made no move for freedom. And as her head tipped back, her lips parted in invitation, he couldn't suppress a groan.

Leaning in, he left a butterfly touch on her lips. It wasn't enough. Electricity flowed out with a snapping connection, starting at the point where they joined, bursting through his body with a jolt. The sensation spread, zapping anything that resembled coherent thought.

He buried his hands in her hair, cupping her head and angling for access.

Sweet and subtle, the taste of her was surprising. He'd expected something indulgent, tropical, like a lazy sunrise morning at the beach. Instead she reminded him of home, of the comfort and stability he'd always craved as a child, with the twinge of something exotic beneath.

Trying to push the errant thought away, he deepened the kiss, opening her mouth with the force of his own and sinking inside.

She made a small mewling sound, loud enough to penetrate the fog of desire and make him pull back. Until he realized it hadn't been a protest. Her hands gripped his shirt, pulling him closer. Her tongue made a foray of its own, tempting, teasing, darting in and out.

Their angles changed again, each of them fighting for a closer, better fit.

He nipped. She bit.

He sucked. She licked.

His world focused and coalesced to one point. The exact space their bodies met.

Suddenly the sound of voices broke through the all-consuming haze, reminding him where they were—a public parking lot. At her office. Where anyone could look out and see Dr. Desire practically sucking a woman whole.

Breaking apart, he registered their bodies, flush in all the right places. Hers pliant and soft everywhere his was rigid. The throbbing pain of denied desire pulsed through his veins and in his temples, and centered at his straining erection.

Taking half a step back, he gave them both the breathing room he desperately needed.

Reaching with a slightly shaky hand, she touched her swollen lips. Her fingers couldn't hide the half smile and pleasant surprise in her eyes.

"I guess you do know what you're doing."

6

KARYN'S BODY HUMMED.

That was some kiss. And she wanted more.

Of course, from the moment she'd set eyes on him, she'd known. Known he could cut through the protective layers she'd built up. Known he could turn her on like no one before. Known that with him nothing else would matter.

And she'd been right.

Not that he seemed to care.

Chris blinked down at her, his eyes glazed with the same arousal still writhing through her body. But as he took another minuscule step away, it became crystal clear he had no intention of a repeat performance.

"What are you afraid of?" The words burst from her like an accusation. Karyn hadn't meant them to be, but…

She was supposed to be the one afraid.

Chris stared. His breath sucked in a little fast, which made something deep inside her…proud. She had done that to him. Clouded his mind, kindled lust in his eyes—and the masculine ridge snuggled next to her body had been hard to miss.

She'd relished the ribbon of awareness that had snaked through her body, heating her senses and leaving a trail of tingling skin in its wake. The feeling was incredible. There was something eternally feminine about it. And powerful.

She'd never felt that kind of passion. Or that desired. She

wanted, no craved, to feel it again. And Chris's sexual interest was unmistakable. So why wouldn't he help her? He wanted her. She needed him. This should have been easy.

His jaw tightened and she knew it wouldn't be easy. "What are you talking about?"

"I know you find me sexually arousing. It was a little hard to miss during our kiss. So why won't you help me?" She moved closer, wondering if she'd had the experience, could she have pushed him over the edge. "You've had countless affairs. All I'd need from you is a few nights."

His body stiffened, and not in the way she wanted.

"Are you afraid of my past? That I'll fall apart on you? Or decide I'm madly in love with you? Or that you won't be able to help me?"

A frown touched his lips. "No. I could help you. I just don't think it's a good idea for either of us."

She reached up, placing a finger to the creases at his brow. "Admit it. You want me."

Karyn didn't know where the words had come from. Or the courage to utter them for that matter. She'd never been sexually forward, not even in her high-spirited teen years, but with Chris it seemed right. The fact that she could put him on edge gave her the tiniest surge of power. She liked the feeling. It was completely different from the lack of control she'd lived with for years. Seductive and tempting, she wanted to feel it again.

"Of course I want you. I'd have to be deaf, dumb and blind not to. You're beautiful. Intelligent. Strong."

He leaned forward and for the briefest moment she wondered if she'd made a tactical error. He was in *her* space now. There was plenty of room to back away, and maybe that's what he wanted her to do, but she didn't. She didn't have to. The unease wasn't there.

"What man wouldn't want to stroke your skin, to discover

how smooth and silky it felt against his rough hands? Or to taste you right before pushing deep inside you?"

Her breath hitched. His whispered words made her sex ache. She'd never been turned on just by words before, but the mental images that flashed through her mind had her thighs clenching together against the slippery proof of her desire to have each of the visions come true. She wanted that. *With him.*

"That's what I'm offering. So what's the problem?"

Her heart squeezed and her skin blushed hot as she realized she'd just propositioned Dr. Desire. Again. Only, this time it hadn't been an accident. She'd meant every last word.

Karyn tilted her face to his, rolling her shoulders back, leaving her neck and chest exposed. Electricity arced between them. She was half-surprised that visible sparks of energy weren't shooting off.

Chris picked up a strand of her hair, sliding it through his fingers before wrapping the ends around his forefinger several times. "You mean aside from the fact that I've promised my boss, my attorney, my producer and you, not to mention myself, that I won't touch you?"

"Is that what you're worried about? No one else needs to know. Not your boss, the attorney, anyone."

She pulled her head to the side, unwinding the strands he still held. She couldn't think while he was playing with her, making her mind go haywire.

"Look, Chris, I haven't felt this way in five years—longer than that if I'm being honest, and I see no reason not to be. I can't explain it. All I know is that while the thought of sex with any other man leaves me cold, the thought of you touching me and coming inside me sends me up in flames."

Her body quivered at the thought of him doing just that with a skittishness she didn't know where she found the inner power to ignore.

She needed him to understand how important this was to her. How much she was willing to sacrifice. Her pride. Her dignity. Anything would be worth taking that last step to freedom and a normal life.

She wanted the chance to find what her oldest brother Randall had. Happiness. Someone she could share her life with. Children to cuddle and to be playmates with her incorrigible niece. But something deep inside her wouldn't let go, would not let her forget and move on.

She didn't know why or how, but Chris made her feel things she hadn't thought possible. He awakened something inside that she'd thought dead. That stupid phone call, those few humiliating minutes she'd wanted to take back, they'd been worth it. Because of him. She could almost taste her future—finally like everyone else's—and see it reflected in his still aroused eyes.

She knew his reputation. Everyone in the city knew. While he refused to talk about his own conquests on air, the women he slept with were all too happy to crow about their experiences with Dr. Desire. And while she sometimes wondered if half of them were true, that didn't matter to her.

She didn't need his notoriety, just his experience, his knowledge—and a few nights from his life.

She had no expectations about the first time. She might have a complete emotional breakdown. But whatever happened, she'd be able to put the experience behind her, locking it away with everything else.

When he left, it would be over and she would move on.

He had to understand. "This is the last step for me. I know in my heart once I get through this first time I'll be fine. You're the link, the bridge between the past and my future. I don't understand it. But I stopped questioning fate a long time ago."

His hand slid from her shoulder to hang at his side. The

distance between them hadn't changed. They were still close enough for the heat of his skin to warm her own. And yet he was withdrawing from her as surely as if he'd gotten in his car and driven away.

Desperation surged up like a shot of adrenaline. She couldn't lose this chance.

"If I'd met you off the street, in a bar, and come on to you, you wouldn't have had a second thought. We'd have been naked within hours. The only thing holding you back right now is my past. The same thing that's been holding me back for five years."

She watched his eyes narrow, hoping the expression meant he saw the truth in her words.

"Whatever you need from me to make this work, just say it. Whatever you're worried about, tell me and we'll work around it. I only want sex. I don't want anything else from you. No need to take me on a date, buy me dinner or send me flowers. Romance not required. Just sex. Whenever you decide you want out, we end it. And I promise never to see you again. Never to try and contact you. Never to call your show. Not even to ask the friend of a friend's cousin how you are. You set any ground rules you want. And when it's over, it's over."

Chris looked down at her, his eyes unreadable. The frown lines were back. She wanted to smooth them away again, but didn't think now was a good time to touch him.

He surprised her by reaching out himself and trailing his index finger gently down her cheek.

"I'll think about it."

SOMETHING CLOSE TO JEALOUSY rolled through Darrell's stomach as he watched his son and the pretty little redhead. He missed the thrill of the chase. The surge of power he got the moment he knew he had a woman in the palm of his hand.

There was nothing like that feeling, when everything coalesced to perfection, when his brilliance and human nature combined to give him whatever he wanted.

And the boy was a chip off the old block. He watched as his son moved in for the kill, pulled a finger down the little girl's cheek and then…walked away?

Maybe the boy didn't know what he was doing after all. Although, listening to his show, he would have thought differently. Maybe the boy lied. Hmm, perhaps he could use that.

The girl stayed right where she was, alone in the parking lot, staring after his son's retreating Porsche. He took a good look at her. Nice legs. Pretty enough face.

She looked familiar though.

He reached across to the passenger seat for the newspaper he'd flung there. Spreading the pages out so that he could get a good look at the picture, he compared her to the grainy black-and-white image of the woman next to his son.

Yep, same one.

The caption named her only as Karyn, a friend of Dr. Desire's. Huh, he'd bet his last fifty bucks they were a hell of a lot more. That kiss had been far from friendly.

But that really didn't concern him. Chris could sleep with whomever he wanted, and more power to him. What he wanted was an angle in, something to convince his son either he was a good guy and deserved a break or something he could hold over his head until the man wrote a check.

Darrell wasn't picky. Either one would do.

Underneath the caption there was a brief story about his son and someone named Katy, a rape victim who'd called into the show last week. He remembered the call and the tizzy Dr. Desire's listeners had been in ever since.

The reporter, Gwen Adair, asked questions, like where the woman was now and why she hadn't come forward despite the public's interest. She practically accused the woman of starting a riot only to duck away because she had something to hide.

The reporter ended the piece with a hint that perhaps the woman in the picture was connected to the call. She stopped short of stating it outright, but the implication was there.

Gazing across the parking lot, Darrell mulled the thought over. Could Karyn be Katy? Honestly, he couldn't care less either way, but the allusion of the story was that if she was, there might be a hell storm of scandal attached to the discovery.

Perhaps Chris would be interested in keeping the truth a secret. Interested enough to pay…

Sinking back into the comfortable leather seat, Darrell watched Karyn walk slowly back into the building. They'd obviously been having a spat when they'd come out. And apparently, she hadn't been left with the warm fuzzies if her demeanor going back inside was anything to judge by.

The skin at the back of his neck prickled. There was something here. At least something worth a few more minutes of his time. It wasn't like he had anything else to do today.

Looking down at his shirt, he realized there was a small stain right below the point of his collar. With a sound of disgust, he jumped out of the car, walked around to the trunk and pulled out a spare shirt from the packed suitcase he'd managed to sweet-talk out of Gloria, Victoria's housekeeper.

He threw the old one down with disgust. He really needed to find someone he could convince to do his laundry. He'd exhausted Gloria's tender feelings.

Using the side mirror, he checked his reflection. It shouldn't take long to get a little background information on Ms. Karyn. All he needed to do was find a receptive woman at the company. If he was lucky, a receptionist on a break.

In his experience, there were a few hard and fast rules when it came to the female race. One was that they loved to listen to themselves chatter. And if what they were droning on about could be considered gossip, they loved it even more.

CHRIS STARED ACROSS his living room at the blank face of his monstrous TV. The game was on. He should have been watching it. Should have had a beer and his buddies there to enjoy it with him.

But that's not how he wanted to spend the night. That's not how he'd wanted to spend the past three nights. He'd wanted to be with her, with Karyn.

He'd imagined her here, everywhere, in the home that he'd built for himself. Sharing the huge bathtub he'd personally tiled. In front of the fireplace he'd repaired. Her legs tight around his waist and her back flush against the walls he'd textured and painted.

Chris had never brought any woman home, had never even envisioned a woman in his space. It was his. He'd worked hard for it, not just the actual blood and sweat he'd shed, but the hours of public appearances, and answering questions on air, and dealing with the headaches of radio life. But every last second of that had been worth it, knowing that this place was his, always his. No one could take it, not even the bank.

Now Karyn was in his head, in his blood *and* in his house. Her words, that voice, that kiss, they all rang inside.

He needed to talk to someone, someone who would understand. Normally Michael was his sounding board, but that was completely out of the question. If he admitted to his producer that he was even considering sleeping with Karyn, his butt would be in the conference room so fast his head would spin. And he'd been there enough lately.

His head dropped back against the leather headrest of his massaging recliner. It had been the latest and greatest thing when he'd been looking for furniture to fill his home. It was comfortable, deep and relaxing. And it only made the fact that there was no one else to call even harder to ignore.

Chris looked around his house, at the state-of-the-art sound system, the wall-mounted television and the sculpture some gallery owner had convinced him was "perfect," and realized he could count the people who had seen it on one hand.

That fact had never bothered him before. In fact, he'd relished the independence and solitude he'd surrounded himself with. Tonight it wasn't enough.

He wanted her here to share it with him.

But that wasn't going to happen.

Jumping up, he stalked through his darkened house, not precisely sure where he was heading until he had his car keys in hand. He'd go for a drive. Clear his head.

He was halfway down the sidewalk to his garage when a movement from the shadows caught his attention.

A man materialized from the darkness. He couldn't tell right away who it was, but the churning anger and disappointment should have been clue enough.

"Where are you heading so late?"

"I'm a little too old for you to start the curfew dance now. You missed those years. And all the others, come to think of it." Chris wanted to continue down the walk, get in his car and drive away, but something made him stay.

He'd seen his father more in the past week than he had his entire life.

"I just thought you might be meeting your latest girl. Wondered if she had a sister."

The urge to wipe the smarmy smile off his father's face was overwhelming. Somehow he found the strength to resist.

"I don't have a girl. And if I did I wouldn't let you in the same zip code with her sister. You aren't getting any money, so you might as well move on to someone else."

The other man shrugged. "I figured that. I admit I was upset, you've got more than you need, but I suppose I can understand. I wanted to know if I could park my car in your driveway for a few nights. I'm living out of it and the cops downtown seem to have gotten wise to me. I'm tired of getting chased away at two in the morning. I'm not getting that much sleep anyway. It's hard to in a two-seater."

Chris closed his eyes, fisted his hands and fought down a brief surge of compassion. This man was a con artist. He knew how to play on human weaknesses, like forgiveness and an instinctive need for a parent's love and approval.

"No. You cannot park your car in my driveway. You cannot have any money. I don't even want to share oxygen with you. Leave. Now."

Darrell held his hands up and let his lips twist in a semi-smile. "I understand. It was worth a try. See you around."

Chris watched his father walk across his rolling green grass to the sporty little Jag at the curb. A twinge of remorse almost made him yell out, but he stopped just in time.

The bastard had made his own bed. Now he could sleep in it.

And if Chris enjoyed the justice that had taken fourteen years to materialize, then that was just a little of his own inner SOB surfacing. At least when his father had condemned *him* to sleep in a car, his mother had owned a nice, big sedan.

KARYN PUTTERED AROUND her kitchen, throwing diced chicken into the sizzling pan and mumbling to herself, "I'm pathetic. That's all there is to it."

There was no other explanation for why she'd turned down Anne's invitation to a Saturday night out in favor of eating alone and brooding.

Last night, during their weekly ritual, her best friend had done nothing but nag. "There's no reason you can't go out with me now. You've been on a date. You said yourself it's time to move on."

But she didn't want to. She had no desire to hit the Birmingham singles' scene with her vivacious friend. She'd never liked the sharp smell of alcohol, overpowering men's cologne and desperation that always permeated those places.

None of it had ever appealed to her under normal circumstances. But add to that the fact that she already knew the man she'd prefer to be with…

And the fact that he'd made it clear he didn't want her? That was what made her pathetic.

Shaking her head, Karyn turned to grab the vegetables she'd chopped when the phone rang. Her heart gave a loud thump against her chest before settling back into place. Jumping every time the thing rang was getting old. Chris was not going to call her out of the blue. Not again.

Grabbing the handset she'd left on the counter, she looked at the caller ID and groaned before answering. She'd begun to think something had happened to her mother; she'd expected this call days ago.

"Hello, Mama. How are you?"

Her mother's voice echoed across hundreds of miles and through thousands of feet of cable. "I'm fine sweetie…now that I know you're not lying in a ditch somewhere." She still had the ability to make her feel like an ungrateful, self-absorbed teenager up to no good.

Karyn fought back a sigh, but let through a smile. Always the same. Her mother had perfected the guilt trip by the time she'd hit five. Karyn knew the habit hid concern for her children, but it had worsened the older they'd gotten.

Her mother had gone into overdrive after the rape. The more media coverage, court dates and accusations she'd gone through, the more smothering her mother had become. She'd tried to talk to her, but it hadn't helped.

"I'm fine, Mama. I know Blake told you that."

"No. What your brother told me was that you probably weren't coming for the family get-together—again. And that you seemed a little depressed—again."

She rolled her eyes. "I am not depressed, Mama, and Blake didn't tell you that. I'm fine. I'm happy. And I said I'd try to come, but couldn't make any promises." Which, she was certain, was exactly the message her brother had passed on.

"You haven't visited in months. I knew this would happen when you moved away. There's no reason you couldn't get a perfectly nice accounting job closer to home."

"Probably. But I like the job I have."

Her mother's harrumph echoed down the line. Karyn smiled; only her mother could put such disappointment and expectation into the sound.

"Do you want to be responsible for ruining everyone's holiday?"

"We're not talking about Christmas. It's Labor Day, for heaven's sake. I'm certain if I don't show up everyone will find the strength to carry on with the hot dogs and beer. I have a lot going on right now—"

The gentle chime of her doorbell cut her off midexcuse.

"Was that your doorbell?"

"Yes, hold on a sec while I get it."

"Don't you open that door for stra—"

Karyn dropped the phone to her side as she walked across her apartment toward the door. She didn't need to hear her mother's admonition about strangers. She'd already had that lesson pounded into her brain with enough force that she'd never forget.

Peeking through the spy hole, Karyn's eyes widened in

shock, and a surge of adrenaline shot through her veins. She blinked just to make sure she'd seen correctly.

Okay, so he hadn't called. Should she take the fact that he'd shown up on her doorstep as a good sign?

Flipping her locks, she decided to open the door and find out.

"Hi."

"Hi." Chris pushed into her apartment. She turned, closed the door and leaned heavily against it. His grim expression did not bode well.

He stood, feet wide apart, planted heavily on her tiled floor, hands fisted to his sides. Every tendon in his body must have been tensed tight because even through his navy T-shirt she could see a muscle jerk in his chest.

Not good.

"All right, I'll sleep with you."

Karyn stared. His stern, serious acceptance wasn't exactly what she'd expected, but a spike of anticipation burst through her nonetheless. The only thing stopping her from throwing her arms around his neck and pulling him into her bed that instant was the expression on his face.

For a man who'd just agreed to sleep with her, he didn't look at all happy about the decision.

She raised her hand to invite him to sit and saw the phone still in her hand. Damn. She'd forgotten about her mother. And she could be certain her overprotective parent had heard every word, because that was the story of her life.

"Uh. Hmm. Make yourself at home." Pointing to the phone, she said, "Give me a minute."

She could hear her mother's voice long before she put the phone back to her ear.

"Who is that? Is that a man's voice? What's going on? Karyn, are you there? Are you okay?"

She supposed she should feel guilty for making her mother worry, because she could tell that she was truly concerned. But she didn't.

"It's just the pizza guy, Mama. I'll talk to you later. I need to pay him."

"Wait. Karyn Michelle Mitchell, did I hear that man say he'd sleep with you? What kind of pizza delivery men do you have over there?"

She laughed at the incredulity and horror in her mother's voice. "No, Mama, he did not offer to sleep with me."

"Well, pay him so he'll leave and we can talk about your trip home."

"There's nothing to talk about. I'll let you know if I'm coming. I've gotta go before my dinner gets cold. Love you."

Not waiting for the inevitable protest, Karyn clicked the off button. She deposited the phone back onto its base and switched off the ringer. The last thing she needed was to hear her mother call back every two minutes while she tried to figure out exactly why Chris was in her living room.

The grim set to his mouth, the tension tightening the already rock-hard muscles and the murky uncertainty in his eyes all told her this wasn't going to be as simple as her visions of them just ripping each other's clothes off, letting him drive her insane before experiencing the best orgasm of her life, and then kissing him goodbye, cured forever of her insecurities and sexual hang-ups.

From where she stood, he looked like the one with the issues, not the other way around.

7

KARYN STARED AT HIM across her modest living room. Chris couldn't read her expression. The urge to twitch seemed to be lodged in every muscle, but somehow he managed not to move while he waited for her reaction. Instead he stood stock-still in the center of her apartment and waited.

He had no idea what he was doing here. He'd gotten in his car, driven around the city and suddenly found he'd pulled into a parking space in front of her apartment.

Sitting there, he'd known he should pull back out again, go home, turn on the game. But something had stopped him. What could it hurt to talk to her? He'd wanted to talk to someone.

And then he'd seen her, framed in the doorway, smelling like peppers and onions, her hair falling from a messy ponytail. And he'd wanted nothing more than to spend the rest of the night in bed making it messier. His big mouth had opened before his brain could stop it.

For the last few days he'd run a litany through his head, a list of reasons why he shouldn't have sex with Karyn. One look at those golden eyes and lush lower lip and he'd forgotten each and every one.

Even with tension filling the air, his blood still hummed with a sexual energy he'd never experienced before. She was half-way across the room, and he ached to close the gap between them and fill his hands with her body.

Yes, she had issues, but all she needed from him was sex. She'd said so herself. He could do this. Sleep with her. He'd done it his whole life, sex for purely physical pleasure. He could help her.

And since he could, wasn't he at least obligated to try? He'd spent the past twelve years of his life regretting the fact that he hadn't been able to do anything for his mother.

What this woman asked of him was simple and, as she'd pointed out, something he'd done a hundred times in his life without thinking. He wanted her almost more than his next breath and she seemed to feel the same. So why not?

"Did you hear me?"

He knew she had. Hell, her mother had.

Karyn shifted on her feet, a gentle rocking motion that drew his attention down to her bright red toenails. It was such a purely feminine touch that his stomach clenched and his balls tightened.

"Why?"

It was a simple question that should have had a simple answer. Instead he stood silent, a jumble of words and thoughts racing through his mind. The encounter with his father. A memory of his mother. His inability to help her when she'd needed him the most.

"Why? Why did you change your mind?"

She stopped, her body ramrod straight, with her back to the kitchen, and the sofa safely between them.

He wasn't the only one contributing to the tension in the room.

He stepped around, moving slowly toward her. Her eyes followed each controlled motion until he was face-to-face with her.

"Because you asked me to." He reached for her, expecting that she might flinch back. But she didn't. Instead she pulled in a deep, deliberate breath and met his gaze.

She didn't say a word—but she didn't have to. He knew her

emotions because he felt a similar jumble inside his own chest. Fear, apprehension, longing. Desire.

His lips tingled with memory and want. Karyn closed her eyes, cutting off his window to her thoughts. But he didn't need them anymore. Taking a strand of her hair between his fingers, he slid the silk through his hand. "Because I can."

She let out a shaky breath and leaned closer. His fingers brushed against the curve of her cheek and she rolled her neck to get nearer.

He wanted to pull her against his body, to press her tight and feel every inch. But something stopped him.

Instead he placed a featherlight kiss on the exposed column of her throat. She tasted sweet and salty. Pulling back, he swiped his tongue across his own lips for another taste.

He wanted more. The tiny moan that whispered through her lips tightened his abdominal muscles. He could pull them both into a sensual haze, surrender to the force that had tugged at them outside her office building.

And yet he hesitated. If he was going to do this, he would do it right. And at this point he wasn't sure what "right" meant. Would it be better to go slow with her? Or to let the frenzy take over and deal with the potential emotional firestorm later?

His stomach clenched again, but this time the rolling waves had nothing to do with sexual desire.

She must have read his hesitancy because her eyes opened, swimming with uncertainty.

"What's wrong?"

"Nothing."

"Changed your mind already?"

Had he? She was giving him the perfect opportunity to back out. He should. Dr. Desire probably would.

"No. But we need to take this slowly. Set some ground rules. Talk."

She laughed. Not precisely what he'd expected.

"What?"

"Talk?"

He saw her smirk, and the tight band constricting his chest eased. "Yes. Talk. You have listened to my show, right? The number-one problem with relationships is lack of communication."

"This isn't a relationship."

"Absolutely. But it isn't as simple as sex, either."

"Sure it is. According to Anne, you're a panty whisperer."

This time he laughed and nearly choked on it. "A what?"

"You know, the kind of guy who could sweet-talk the panties off any woman with a pulse."

"I'm not sure I like that." In fact, that analogy hit a little too close to home, reminding him strongly of his father.

Sure, he'd had his share of sexual partners. But he'd never been malicious about it or selfishly gratifying. Now, Darrell, that man used sex as a way to get whatever he wanted and didn't care who got hurt in the process.

His mother was the perfect example.

Karyn laid a hand on his arm. "I'm sorry I didn't—"

Damn. He really needed to get his father out of his mind. The man was seriously screwing with his head.

"It's nothing."

Taking her by the hand, he pulled them both around to the sofa and pushed her gently down into one corner.

"Ground rules. No one else knows. This is to protect you, as well as me."

She nodded. "Trust me. The last thing you need to worry about is me running to the local TV station for an interview."

Chris cocked his head at her sarcastic tone. There was something beneath those words, something he'd explore later. Maybe.

"I need you to promise you'll do exactly what I say. If you

don't like something, say so, but other than that no questioning my methods." Not that he had any. Yet.

She swallowed, and he wondered if she was doubting herself. Or him.

"I need you to be absolutely sure this is what you want, Karyn. We both need to be able to trust each other. You're putting your body in my hands, and I'm putting my career in yours."

She studied him for several moments. His heart seemed to thump louder and louder as the seconds ticked by. Her tongue darted out across her lips before she sucked the bottom one into her mouth and worried it with her teeth.

He stared back and tried not to let any of his second—or third—thoughts show on his face. The last thing she needed was to realize he wasn't sure about this.

"I have a rule of my own."

"What is it?"

"No past. I don't want to talk or think about what happened. If you need to know anything, ask now, because after tonight those moments will be behind me forever."

He considered. Her request was completely understandable. He couldn't see any reason to have the details. To be honest, he really didn't want them.

"I don't think I need specifics, just if there's something I should avoid."

She blinked, and her entire expression changed. Hope flashed through her eyes, followed by a heat that singed him and kindled an answering fire deep in his gut.

She leaned toward him, grabbed his face and fused her mouth to his. It was nothing like that moment by his car. There was too much fear and desperation behind this kiss.

Even so, his body reacted.

She thought he meant now.

Framing her face, he changed the angle of the kiss and

gentled it. He nudged her back slowly, then pulled away. Taking her hand, he urged her up from the sofa and headed toward the door, leading her behind him.

"Where are you going?" Her voice came out as a raspy whisper. His muscles tensed as her hand touched his back; an answering ripple pulled his spine tight. One touch, not even a sexual one and he was ready to implode.

"Home." He tried to keep the need for her from his voice.

"Home? We aren—"

Her mouth slammed shut so hard he heard her teeth grind together.

"Nope. Not tonight."

He had a phone call to make. Homework. He might not have spoken to his college roommate in years, but the man had been a psych major and had a thriving practice in Montgomery. Chris knew his way around a woman's body, but he'd be the first to admit he understood little about their minds. Oh, he put on a good show on the air, but in reality…

Something told him he'd need to know all aspects of a woman if he wanted to help her.

He was going to do this right.

Karyn deserved that.

KARYN SLUMPED into her big, stuffed chair and clutched the throw pillow to her stomach. Dr. Desire had just agreed to have sex with her.

She wasn't precisely sure what to feel. Excited. Terrified. Aroused.

He'd agreed to sleep with her. And then walked out her door, leaving her alone with the hum of anticipation flowing through her blood.

But it was finally going to happen.

After years of fear, years of resigning herself to unsatisfying nights with a vibrator, she was going to experience sex again. Amazing sex. With the hottest man in Birmingham.

As long as the anxiety didn't resurface.

As long as he didn't change his mind.

HE WAS HAVING second thoughts. Twenty and thirty thoughts if the truth be told.

Chris eased back into the desk chair in his office and looked out the window into the busy hallway.

Normally he'd be at home, in bed, at this ungodly hour of the morning. Ten o'clock might not be early for most people, but it was for him.

Saturday night he hadn't been able to sleep. First thing Sunday morning, he'd called his college roommate. He hadn't spoken to Paul in years, but that hadn't seemed to bother his old friend. They'd talked for quite some time about Karyn and her situation. Paul had convinced him to trust that she knew what she needed and had recommended a book about recovering from sexual abuse. He'd bought it immediately and had been racing through it, trying to nail down a game plan before contacting Karyn. There was no doubt; he'd be consulting it frequently and he wasn't even halfway through.

He squinted down at the page with tired, gritty eyes. Dr. Walker's book was good and intimidating. Just reading the slow and steady steps the doctor suggested… Pressure had built behind his eyes and tightened every muscle in his body.

This wasn't going to be as simple as he'd first thought. Yes, he'd known they'd need to take special precautions to ensure Karyn's comfort. But nothing like the methodical steps suggested in the book. He'd never thought about sex in such a clinical fashion.

The first step the book recommended was nonsexual touches. Chris hoped their dinner at Masquerade counted because he didn't think he could touch her without any intent behind the caress. Besides, Karyn hadn't seemed to have a problem with the sensual touches they'd shared so far, so he figured maybe she'd already moved past that point.

The second step was personal sexual touches. He couldn't touch her and she couldn't touch him. Dr. Walker suggested both people unclothe for this step, but he wasn't sure he'd be able to do that. Karyn might trust him, but he didn't trust himself. He figured he'd ask her what she wanted. If she'd be more comfortable with him naked, then he'd do it. And tie his hands to a chair if he had to.

After that he had more torture to look forward to, in the form of actually touching her without intercourse. How was he supposed to manage that? Tying his hands wouldn't be an option.

Chris looked down at the pad of legal paper beside him. He had a page and a half of notes. Notes. On how to have sex. There was something supremely wrong with this picture.

But if he was going to do this, he was going to follow Dr. Walker's suggestions to the letter. Maybe once he felt confident that he knew what he needed to do for Karyn, he'd stop hearing the little voice inside his head that kept saying, *You're going to screw this up.*

The fact that the voice in his head sounded just like his father wasn't helping much, either.

Chris rubbed his hands over his face, the prickly stubble he hadn't bothered to shave scratching his skin. At least the man hadn't been loitering outside his house when he got home last night. He should be glad for small favors.

"What are you doing here?"

Chris jumped, the jolt of hearing Michael's voice enough to stop his heart cold for a second or two. His panicked gaze flew to the book open on his desk. If his producer could read the spine, it wouldn't take him long to figure out what was going on.

"Just catching up on some reading. Making some notes."

He nonchalantly closed the book, turning it facedown with the spine covered, careful to tuck his legal pad beneath.

Michael narrowed his eyes. Chris met his friend's skeptical gaze and tried not to blink.

"What's going on, Chris?" Shutting the door behind him, Michael slouched down into the office chair across from his desk. "I don't think I've ever seen you here this early on a Monday morning."

"I needed to get out of my place for a little while."

"Okay, now I know something's wrong. That house is your hidey-hole. You go *there* to get away, not to the station. How many times have you complained that you can't get anything done up here because of the interruptions?"

All the time. And normally it was the truth. The minute he stepped into the station someone wanted his attention. The marketing department wanted to set up another appearance or photo shoot or one of the sponsors needed him to record a new spot…

Today everyone had left him alone. Everyone but Michael.

"Nothing's wrong. I just needed a change of scenery this morning. And so far you're the only one who's bothered me."

Michael sighed, ignoring the hint. "You're not still tied up over Katy, are you? I know you weren't happy about that picture, but I thought you'd talked to her about it, that she was fine."

"She is. It is. I haven't thought about her in days." Chris held steady on Michael's eyes, knowing if he so much as breathed funny his producer would be on him like white on rice.

"Then what's wrong?"

"I'm just tired, a little stressed."

"It's no wonder. You've been doing quite a bit of publicity lately. And with this Katy stuff… When's the last time you took a vacation?"

"I don't need a vacation."

"Everyone needs a chance to blow off some steam now and again, Chris. There's nothing wrong with taking a break from your real life. Go somewhere no one knows you, have a fling. You'll come back feeling like a new man."

"Yeah, maybe."

Standing, Michael headed toward the door. "Trust me."

Chris crossed his arms over the notepad and book. Maybe.

Getting out of the city might be good for Karyn. It couldn't hurt him, either. It would certainly lessen his odds of being recognized, freeing them up to enjoy their time together with one less complication.

It might also have the added benefit of loosening her up.

The more he thought about Michael's idea the better he liked it. What would Dr. Walker say about leaving behind the real world in favor of a weekend getaway? What step would that be?

DARRELL WAITED in the dark parking lot outside Dr. Desire's flagship radio station. His head dropped back against the soft, buttery leather as blaring rock music filled the space. He hated this kind of music, it was more noise than talent if you asked him, but he needed to wait until Chris's show came on before he could make his move.

He had no idea what he expected to find in his son's office, but it had been a piece of cake to swipe the entrance card from the bubbly receptionist he'd spoken to this morning. He had access, so why not?

Besides, you just never knew what small piece of information would be the clue to unlocking someone's deepest desires or strongest fears. Once you knew either of those two things you had them by the short and curlies.

His mother's death was obviously a sore point with Chris,

but he had yet to figure out how to use that to his advantage in this situation. If anything, it worked against Darrell.

How the boy could blame him for his mother's cancer was beyond him, but he obviously did. It wasn't like the bitch had told him the money was to pay hospital bills and rent so they could keep their house.

Not that it would have mattered. Joy had made her decision, just like he had, and she'd lived with the consequences. Of course, at the moment Darrell was grateful she hadn't aborted their son. If she had, who knew what would have happened to him now? Chris was his ticket back to comfort and the place in this world he was rightfully owed.

At nine o'clock on the dot, Chris's voice filled the cramped Jag. "We have a great show lined up for tonight. I hope everyone's ready for some tantalizing fun."

It was time.

Taking out the nondescript white card, Darrell walked into the building, went to the doorway at the far end of the reception area, the same one he'd watched countless people walk through this morning, and swiped it through the reader. With a quiet beep and a loud click, the lock let go and he opened the door.

Walking into the radio station beyond, it took him a while to navigate through several stories of offices, storage closets, computer and telephone rooms and broadcast booths before he found what he was looking for. While the spaces he passed weren't run-down, they weren't exactly the high-tech meccas he'd expected, either. Everything was neat and tidy, but somehow the plain beige walls and spotless glass just wasn't what he'd pictured.

Not that it mattered.

The place was nearly deserted. Every once in a while he heard the lone sound of a footstep here or there, a voice that seemed to be talking to no one in particular.

It didn't take him long to find Dr. Desire's office. Not the biggest, it had a decent view, was off a hallway by itself and seemed nice and remote. Which made his job easier.

He had no idea if Chris came to his office during breaks. He tended to think not, but you never knew. The faster he looked around the better.

Slipping inside, he took a quick, cursory glance. He perused the bookshelf that sat against a far wall, noting with some warped sense of fatherly pride the lines of awards and plaques.

Finding nothing important, he quickly turned to Chris's desk. Sitting down into his chair, Darrell enjoyed the gentle creak of well-worn leather and the expensive smell that enveloped him.

Flipping on the computer sitting on the desk, he groaned when after a few minutes it booted up, but blinked angrily at him, requesting a password. He could make a guess, several educated ones probably, but he didn't really have that kind of time right now.

Shutting the machine down, he opened drawers and started riffling through files and junk instead. Nothing major popped out at him.

Closing everything, he placed his hands on the desktop and took one long, hard stare around just to make sure he hadn't missed anything. He'd hate for this exercise to be a complete bust—although it had been a long shot to begin with.

He was about to get up and leave when his gaze swung down to the slightly cushy surface beneath his hands. A desk blotter calendar.

Darrell looked over the big, mostly blank squares. Here and there a few things were written in scrawling letters that reminded him eerily of his own atrocious handwriting. Most people couldn't read anything he wrote, which could come in handy when he wanted it to.

But he could read Chris's notes with little effort. Most of them were appearances, appointments for the station. Here and there were ideas for show topics he wanted to cover. What caught Darrell's attention was the upcoming weekend. While nothing had been written on any other Saturday or Sunday, both of those days for this week had been marked off and Morgan-ville scrawled in large letters between the two.

So his son was going out of town for the weekend.

He wondered if the little redhead would join him.

BUTTERFLIES FLUTTERED inside her stomach as Karyn slipped the last of her new lingerie into her suitcase and zipped it shut.

"Am I doing the right thing?"

Karyn sat on the bed next to her bag and looked at Anne. Her friend had come over to help her choose what to pack and for an abbreviated version of girls' night.

"Of course you are."

"Then why am I nervous?"

Anne came and sat on the bed beside her. "Because you're human. This is a big step for you, Karyn. Yes, I think you need this, but that doesn't mean it's going to be easy."

Flopping back on the bed, the suitcase rocked against her hip. "I just want this over." She rolled her head to look at Anne. "I'm so tired of dealing with the rape. I moved to Birmingham to put it all behind me, for a fresh start." She sighed and stared back at the ceiling. "But the problems I had at home just followed me."

"They usually do. But you're doing something about it." Anne jumped from the bed, grabbed her by the arms and pulled her up. "Now, stop second-guessing yourself. I'd kill for a free weekend getaway. Enjoy it, girl!"

Karyn smiled and shook her head.

"And if you get there and decide you've made a mistake, you can always dump him and hit the shops. I hear they're cute and quaint. Of course, it would be a shame to waste all that new silk and lace."

Her friend's eyes twinkled with mischief, and Karyn felt a twinge of envy. Why couldn't she be more like Anne? Throw caution to the wind and let the past be damned?

"Just do me one favor."

"I will not give you a blow-by-blow."

"No. Just don't fall in love."

"I have no intention—"

Anne stared at her, the sparkle gone. "You say that now, but you haven't had sex in a long, long time. Take if from someone who's broken her share of hearts—it's easy to confuse good sex with emotional attachment."

With a sigh, Karyn made a promise she heartily hoped she could keep. Developing feelings for Chris would be the worst thing that could happen, for so many reasons. Their agreement would only last for a few days and then it would be over and a new chapter in her life would begin.

Surely she'd be so caught up in taking this step there'd be no room for her heart to get involved.

She and Anne joked, shared their normal pizza, devoured the ice cream and listened to Chris's show for the next few hours. Anne left around eleven, leaving her alone in the dark with her butterflies.

A shiver snaked down her spine as Chris told his listeners good-night in that dark, raspy voice. She hoped her night would be much more than good. Her breasts tingled as her imagination kicked in.

That sensation alone reassured her. In the five years since her rape only Chris had sparked that immediate physical response in her body.

If things moved according to plan they'd be on the road by twelve-thirty, there around three and in bed together by 3:05.

Tonight it would be over. And the rest of the weekend she could enjoy having the sexiest man in Birmingham in her bed.

Her heart jerked at the soft knock on her front door a half hour later. She took a deep breath, grabbed the small case and headed to Chris.

She opened the door wide. He leaned down out of the shadows into the light and placed a warm kiss to her cheek. The spot burned, and her lips parted in an unconscious plea for more.

"Are you ready to go?"

She nodded.

"I'm sorry we're leaving at such a weird hour, but I thought it might be better to go ahead and get there so we'd have the full two days to enjoy Morganville."

The only thing she planned to enjoy for the next two days was him. But she thought better of stating that.

He slung her bag over his shoulder, and they headed for a dark gray SUV that was more functional than the red speed demon.

"It usually takes me a few hours to wind down after a show, anyway, so I don't mind the drive. You should sleep, though."

Her whole body flushed at the implication as he smiled across the SUV's dark interior. Was that intent in his eyes? She couldn't tell but her body sure thought so.

They were miles down the road before she finally relaxed into the soft leather seats and her eyelids began to droop. Out on the highway it wasn't long before the dark night and hypnotic motion lulled her to sleep. It felt as if they'd just left when his soft voice woke her. "Karyn. We're here."

She fought off the groggy feel of interrupted sleep and rolled her neck to fight a cramp. Chris stood beside her open door, the light from a streetlamp at his back gilding his rich, dark hair and hiding his face in shadow.

But she felt his eyes, could see the glitter of them even in the darkness.

Her breath caught and heat rushed in. The only thought in her brain: *finally.*

As if sensing her reaction, he took a giant step away, leaving a gaping space between them.

"I've already checked us in."

Turning on his heel, he picked up the bags she hadn't noticed at his feet and walked to the front door of a charming little cabin.

She stood outside for a moment, allowing the predawn air to cool her skin and blow away the cobwebs still in her head.

It was adorable, perfectly Southern. A tiny log cabin with worn wooden rockers, hand-hooked rugs and an old-fashioned porch swing crowded onto the wraparound deck.

Following him to the front door he held open, she walked inside. She looked up into his face as she passed by and the butterflies returned full force. But overriding them was a fizzing in her veins like the exploding bubbles in a freshly opened can of cola.

The place was small and quiet, made up of two rooms—a combined living room/kitchen and a bedroom. It carried the smell of an old, loved house—a mixture of beeswax, disinfectant and slightly musty wood.

The small touches—a patchwork quilt, a vase of blooming red roses, a china cabinet full of a blue willow pattern—left the impression that she'd stepped into someone's treasured home.

"It's perfect." Not an impersonal hotel room or a bed-and-breakfast with paper-thin walls. It was homey and safe. Just what she'd needed. She had no idea how he'd known. She hadn't.

Turning, she meant to hug Chris, to thank him for finding this place, but instead of standing behind her like she'd expected, he was still in the doorway staring in.

"I hope you like it. I'll put your things on the couch. Breakfast is in the main cabin up the hill at eight, but I know it's pretty late. So sleep as long as you want, we'll grab something when you wake up."

He deposited her bags and then moved back out onto the porch. "Pleasant dreams."

He was down the steps before her tongue would work. "Wait. You're not staying here with me?"

He turned, but didn't come back. "I didn't think that would be a good idea."

"But—"

"I want you to be comfortable, Karyn. I'm in the cabin next door. It's late."

She could feel the anger and disappointment rising.

He must have seen them both because with an animal grace-fulness that sent her pulse fluttering, he bounded back up the porch steps to her side.

"You agreed to follow my rules, Karyn. And right now this one's hard and fast."

With an intensity that made her knees buckle, Chris scooped her into his arms, kissed her hard enough to make the stars spin and then set her gently back on the ground with a whispered "Good night."

Her tongue felt heavy and useless as she watched him dis-appear through the darkness into the cabin next door. A light flickered on inside, illuminating the blue gingham curtains pulled tight against the night.

Comfortable? Not likely. Not when her blood hummed with expectation.

Good night? Not anymore.

8

CHRIS HUGGED his cup of coffee and stared out over the porch railing at the early-morning haze. He hadn't slept, not much anyway. It had been difficult knowing Karyn was only a few yards away, in that cabin all by herself.

He shifted, trying to relieve the pressure behind his jeans. He was actually getting pretty used to walking around with a perpetual hard-on. Not that he particularly enjoyed the sensation. Unfortunately, he'd have to live with it for a little while longer.

Today the agenda included watching Karyn masturbate—no touching allowed. The thought of watching her touch herself was erotic as hell. The realization that he couldn't do anything about it, not so much.

"Good morning."

Karyn's voice jolted through his system, much stronger than the caffeine he'd been using to jumpstart his brain. He needed every last ounce of intelligence and willpower so he wouldn't do something stupid—like bypass straight to the sex and screw this up for them both.

He turned at the rail, leaning back against it as she slid beside him. "You're up early. I expected you to sleep the morning away."

Leaning out over the weather-smoothed wood, she turned and gave him a perfect morning smile. "Nope. I'm pretty much a morning person. Besides, I found it difficult to sleep."

"Why?"

She shot him a pointed look through lowered lashes. "Knowing you were next door was a bit distracting. Besides, I'd worked up this whole fantasy in my head about how last night would end."

Reaching over, she snagged his cup and sipped. "Hmmm, that's good. But it needs more sugar."

She returned the cup, taking his hand and sandwiching it between the warm, heavy china and the heat of her palm.

Shifting her body next to his, she looked up, a gold glint in her eyes. "So, are you coming back to bed with me?"

Chris studied her. Karyn was a walking, talking contradiction, strong on one hand, vulnerable on the other. Undeniably sexy, part of her magnetism stemmed from the fact that she seemed mostly oblivious to it. And while he enjoyed a sexually forward woman as much as the next guy, the woman who'd just walked up beside him and bluntly asked him to bed did not fit the Karyn he'd gotten to know over the last few days.

The way she was looking up at him, her body touching his from shoulder to thigh, reminded him of every other woman who'd come on to him just to sleep with Dr. Desire. She'd never seemed to fit that mold before.

Yet there was a slight tremor in the hand still cupping his.

"No." The word was painful to say. At the moment there wasn't much he could think of wanting more.

"What do you mean?" She straightened suddenly, spilling drops of coffee across their still-joined hands. She let go of the cup, and him, to suck away the brown liquid.

He watched her plush lips open, close, and felt their pull on the spot between her thumb and forefinger deep inside. His fist tightened around the warmed ceramic. It wasn't what he wanted to hold.

She stood before him, a deflated angel with red wisps and

dark golden eyes. Her face was fresh, her skin pink and glowing in the early-morning sun. His chest tightened. He wanted to touch her. But he couldn't. Not and keep his promise to them both.

"We only have two days." She stepped closer, the curve of her breast deliberately brushing his arm. "I don't want to waste any of it."

Her blatant come-on *was* sexy; he couldn't remember a time he'd been more aroused. But it wasn't real. He knew that. Karyn might think she was ready to jump straight into bed with him, but she wasn't. What she needed was some time to adjust to the idea. To get used to him.

Hell, they'd barely spent five hours together. She couldn't trust him, not yet, and Dr. Walker said trust was important.

According to the good doctor, lack of trust between the rape victim and her partner could lead to any number of disasters, all of which he really wanted to avoid. For her sake and his.

"We have two days to enjoy ourselves, Karyn." Chris cupped her chin and ran the pad of his thumb against the swell of her lower lip. "We need to take our time. Build trust. There's no rush."

"Yes, there is. I can taste freedom. I want it, Chris." She looked up into his eyes. "I've never wanted anything more."

He wanted *her*. This second. But he wouldn't, couldn't take her. Not yet. Maybe not even this weekend, if he couldn't trust himself to stay in control.

Pushing away from her with more force than he'd intended, Chris stepped backward, the railing catching him hard across the back.

"Rules, remember. You agreed to do exactly what I say. Ever been horseback riding?"

"Horseback rid— What does that have to do with anything?"

"I picked up a brochure in the lobby this morning. I thought you might like to go. If you're not afraid of horses."

"Mississippi girl, remember? Riding is not a problem. I just didn't plan on doing it on a horse this weekend."

Chris gulped down the swallow of coffee he'd taken. He looked hard at her over the cup. Her face was perfectly bland.

"Great." He'd been busy this morning making plans for the weekend—a trip to the lake, a hot-air balloon ride, a romantic dinner in her cabin. If things went well, step two would be marked off the list tonight.

Maybe between staying busy and following the steps, he could keep his hands off her.

He'd never been in this situation before, facing a willing woman he also wanted and denying himself—them both. Yes, in the past he'd chosen his women carefully—they'd had to understand the ground rules—but then if they'd been interested, he'd been willing.

Karyn might understand the ground rules, but there was more at stake this time than just making sure she had multiple orgasms.

At the moment he sincerely hoped a few hours in a saddle would cool his jets. Because his self-control was about to snap.

DARRELL CRUNCHED farther down into the passenger seat of his Jag. Why couldn't the bitch hurry up? He'd been waiting here for almost an hour. His back was killing him.

Finally his pain and patience were rewarded. A woman with stooped shoulders and short silver curls emerged from Chris's front door, crossed the perfect green lawn separating the yards and walked up to her own place.

She didn't even glance around as she shut her door behind her.

He'd spoken to the woman earlier, tried to convince her that he needed access to his son's home. She hadn't believed him. *She* was the one Chris asked to watch his house and water the plants.

Standing in her flower-filled, ruffle-covered parlor—her

word not his—he'd briefly entertained a vision of wrapping his hands around her paper-thin throat and squeezing. She was so frail. He could have easily taken the key.

But he had already prepared a backup plan. Much better to wait until she'd come and gone and then simply let himself inside. It wouldn't take much to break through the lock on the back door. He just hoped he could figure out the code to the alarm system his son surely owned.

Grabbing a shiny silver tube of lipstick and a pair of rubber gloves from the glove compartment, he sat in impatient silence. He had a plan to throw everyone off track, something even his son would believe. A light finally snapped on in a second-story room next door, telling him it was time to go.

Darrell slipped from his car, ignoring the creaking in his knees and ankles, and casually walked up the drive, across the yard and around to the back gate. No one tried to stop him. Hell, no one even cared.

Within thirty seconds he was at Chris's back door. Pulling on the gloves, he grabbed a stick from the yard and jammed it hard into the tiny rectangular window midway up the door. It shattered with a sound far louder than he'd expected. But he didn't have time for the surprise to slow him.

Almost immediately, the alarm began beeping a warning. Reaching inside, he twisted the lock and dead bolt, flung the door open and ran to the control panel mounted at the far end of the narrow hallway.

He'd expected this and he'd come up with a list of numbers he thought Chris might use. Most people didn't like numbers, and they really didn't like to memorize a slew of different ones. Passwords, pins, codes. Human nature was to choose several you could remember—birthdays, anniversaries—and rotate them around.

While he'd waited, Darrell had racked his brain and come

up with a few he knew. Punching in Chris's birthday, he held his breath and waited. Nothing. His mother's birthday didn't disarm it, either. Darrell's heart pounded in his ears. Hot adrenaline swamped his system.

Then he tried one more. He didn't really think his son would choose this date but…

No one had told him the day Chris's mother had died. No one had thought he would care. But Chris had been three weeks from his eighteenth birthday so child services had contacted him as the father to let him know that his son was now alone. They'd advised him that Chris had petitioned against foster care. Since he would have been free to leave weeks later, anyway, and he'd shown the capability to support himself, they'd allowed him to live on his own. But they'd thought Darrell might want to know.

He hadn't. At the time, there wasn't anything he could have done for the boy. And besides, he'd turned out fine. He was living in this fancy house. Had thousands of fans who adored him and a radio station that thought he walked on water.

Darrell punched seven, two, four, nine, four and felt a bead of sweat roll down his back. His heart squeezed tight as the last number registered. And the panel beeped acceptance and shut itself off.

Sagging against the opposite wall, Darrell let his head fall backward and his eyes close. Why would his son choose that date?

Yes, he'd felt bad. For Joy. No, their relationship hadn't ended the way either of them had wanted… Joy had been different from every other woman in his life. Young, just out of high school, she hadn't had a penny to her name. Normally that would have been a deal breaker for him, but he'd been young, too. And mesmerized—for a while. She'd been beautiful and sweet…innocent. Naive, as well, it turned out.

Shaking away the unpleasant memories and the tight ache in his chest, Darrell pushed away from the wall to close the door.

He looked around his son's dark, cool space, from the huge television to the entire wall of electronics, the leather sofas and reclining chairs, the modern artwork that almost covered a wall, and felt his temper rise. The boy had everything he could possibly want. And he wouldn't spare a little for the man who'd given him life.

Well, he would just see about that. He walked to the stocked liquor cabinet, pulled out an expensive bottle of Scotch and poured himself several fingers. Glass in hand, he moved slowly through the house, looking for anything he could use. Account numbers, credit cards, documents, anything he could turn into cash.

The place was full of electronics…he could probably fence them for money to get through the next few days. But it wouldn't be nearly enough for what he needed to set up the appearance of an affluent lifestyle. That required a rather large chunk of disposable funds.

He'd been at it for an hour, working methodically through room after room with nothing to show for it when he walked into a spare bedroom at the end of the upstairs hall. His son had turned it into an office—huge desk, wall of awards, two computers.

He sat in Chris's chair, the dark brown leather protesting his intrusion. Pulling drawer after drawer, he hunted for account records, bank statements, anything, but found nothing.

He came up empty at the book shelves, as well. In a last-ditch effort, he upturned the wire mesh trash can sitting between a shelf and the credenza. Several white pages floated out onto the ground followed by an empty paper coffee cup and a bag from a local doughnut place.

The rubbish he ignored. The papers he picked up, scanning them quickly. The first two appeared to be printouts from a Web site and held nothing important. The last one, though, caught his attention.

It was a reservation for this weekend at a place called Hidden Mountain Cabins in Morganville. He was missing the first page—it wasn't in the trash can—but he did have an address.

A giddy sense of excitement washed over him. He wasn't sure what he could do with the information, but he was certain a few more hits from Chris's liquor cabinet would help him figure it out.

But before he did that, he had one more thing to do.

Walking through his son's bedroom, Darrell headed for the attached bathroom. The space was larger than the car he was currently living in. His eyes lingered on the huge walk-in shower, big enough for five people to fit comfortably. It had been so long since he'd had a decent shower…the temptation was almost too much.

The dirty towels would be pretty hard to hide, though.

Tearing his gaze away, he went over to the sink and picked up the navy blue toothbrush sitting in a stand and put it into one pocket. Next, he pulled out the lipstick he'd stashed in the other, uncapped the tube and wrote a nice message for his son.

Just a few memories,
Your #1 fan

Stepping back, he admired the effect of the bright red against the slick silver surface.

Walking back through the bedroom he stopped at the closet, opened the door and searched for something else, something small. Spying the laundry hamper, he smiled. Digging inside, he pulled out every pair of underwear.

KARYN SPENT the day alternating between aroused and relaxed. They'd had a fantastic day filled with two glorious hours walking and trotting through pastures and a small forest, browsing little shops, enjoying a museum of natural oddities and more laughter than she could remember.

He'd bought her a stupid little glass penguin. She'd admired it in a shop, the light catching its cute little wings and drawing her over to touch. Two minutes later they'd been walking out with the thing wrapped in layers of tissue. It wasn't important or expensive, but it had made her heart constrict when he'd handed her the bag.

It would be a memory of their weekend together.

While he wasn't looking, she'd slipped back into a store and purchased a ridiculously expensive pair of cuff links he'd looked at. All things considered, they were hardly enough, but she wanted to have something to give him when this was all over, something to let him know how important this was for her, how much she appreciated his help.

Last night had not been fun. Dreaming about him, wanting his touch, his hands on her body. She had absolutely no intention of letting this evening end with him disappearing down that gravel walk. This would be the night if she had to tie him to the bed and seduce the pants off of him—literally. She might not know what she was doing but she was a quick study. She'd figure it out.

Karyn looked at her face in the mirror one last time, tweaked a strand of hair till it fell obediently into place and tried to banish the twitchy flutters inside. She wanted this. There was no need for nerves.

Tonight it would be all over—the pressure, the waiting, the loneliness.

A knock sounded on the door. She jumped up, tugged at the

hem of her summer sweater and wondered if the hot-pink thong she'd put on was a little too much. Anne had sworn any man would swallow his tongue over it. Now that she had it on under her skin-tight jeans, she wasn't so sure.

She definitely wasn't used to the sensation, especially the cool feel of the rhinestone-studded string against her skin.

But Karyn was ready to dive headfirst into this experience. She'd been looking forward to it for days, weeks, years. The twisting sensation was not nerves. There was nothing to be nervous about. They'd have sex and she'd be fine.

With a steadying breath, she opened the door, expecting to find Chris. Instead a knot of people stood on her front porch. She counted three, all carrying bags and boxes. An enticing aroma filled the air: spices, peppers, ripe tomatoes.

"Good evening. We're here to set up dinner." The man in front spoke with a slight accent she couldn't place, and waited for her to move.

It took her a few moments to realize what he needed. "Oh. Sure, come in." She backed away from the door, watching as the group filed into the tiny kitchen and set to work.

In no time flat they had a tablecloth, lit candles, two place settings and several covered platters filling the small table in a nook. Dusk was falling outside the surrounding windows. Fireflies winked against the backdrop of rolling foothills.

"Good evening."

The efficient army filed past her once again and out the door. She stared after them, the wafting aroma the only irrefutable evidence that they'd really been there. Her stomach growled. And then he was there. Standing, framed in the doorway of her little cabin.

He'd taken a shower. His hair gleamed damp in the porch light that had winked on as the sun fell. He wore a faded pair of jeans. They looked soft and comfortable, her favorite kind.

A navy blue polo, opened at the neck, revealed a few swirls of dark hair.

She couldn't help but contrast him to the man who'd met her for dinner less than two weeks ago. That man had been slick, packaged, sexy. This one…he was relaxed, comfortable, perfect—and sexy.

She couldn't fight the feeling that today Chris had shown her a side of himself he let very few people see. The world knew him as Dr. Desire, the man who knew everything, could charm anyone, was cool, calm and confident.

How many people saw the real Chris? The man behind the public persona? She wasn't sure she had, but thought she was getting close.

"Good. Dinner's here. I thought I saw the delivery van outside."

He walked in, stopped at her side to press a kiss to her lips, then let her go before it really started. Her tongue darted out, the taste of him mixing with the aromas in the air.

Her blood rushed hot before slowing to a molten pace in her veins. Dinner. She had to get through dinner first.

"What is all this?"

She walked up to the table behind Chris as he began uncovering dish after dish. Refried beans. Guacamole. Chips, salsa, chicken fajitas.

"Mexican. You said it was your favorite."

When he'd asked her this afternoon, she'd thought he'd just been playing the getting-to-know-you game. She hadn't realized he'd actually been paying attention. She fought down a grin as it teased at the edges of her lips and tried not to be charmed.

Then Karyn looked over at Chris and couldn't help it. He had a mischievous grin of his own. Okay, so she was charmed. What was the harm in that?

"Good boy." She patted him on the head and tried to

dislodge the feeling of utter happiness that had spiked into her heart.

Chris hadn't done this because he cared…okay, well, maybe he did, but not in the way that mattered. He hadn't ordered her favorite foods because he'd wanted to make her feel special and cherished. He'd wanted her to feel comfortable, to be at ease so this experience would go smoothly for them both.

As romantic dinners went it shouldn't have ranked. Rolled tortillas dripping sour cream and cheese everywhere shouldn't have been sexy. But they were, with Chris. She'd bet the man had the ability to turn scrubbing soap scum sexy.

With a laugh, he swiped a disastrous drip from the bottom of her fajita and offered it to her. Without thinking, she opened her mouth and took it in, enjoying the cool taste of sour cream and the salty tang of his skin against her tongue. And then a jolt of electricity hit. She swallowed, sucking harder on his finger and brought her gaze to meet his.

The laughter between them froze, suspended, the physical contact bringing them back to reality. They *were* enjoying themselves. But the joking and camaraderie was a flimsy veneer over the anticipation and nerves underneath.

Chris pulled his finger gently from her mouth. Part of her wanted to hold tight and part of her wanted to let him go.

"Would you do something for me if I asked?"

Would she? "Probably. What do you want?"

"Will you touch yourself for me?"

A hot blush surfed up her cheeks. "Why?"

He sat back in his chair, widening the space between them. His intent gaze kept the thread of awareness from snapping. "It's a sexual connection between us that doesn't involve actual sexual contact."

"I don't think that's necessary."

"I do."

She tried not to be embarrassed—the emotion seemed a bit misplaced considering what she'd asked of him—but she couldn't help it. He deserved her honesty, no matter how uncomfortable it made her. "I've spent five years touching myself, Chris. I don't want to do it anymore. That's why I asked you for help."

"And I'm trying to give it to you. We need to build trust, Karyn. You're placing your body in my hands. You need to know it's a good decision."

"It is."

He shifted in his chair. "You agreed to do what I asked. This is important, Karyn, and we're not going any further until we accomplish it."

Her mind raced and she turned away. It would be embarrassing. But if that was her only objection…a little discomfort would be worth it in the end, if this worked and she was cured.

"Look at me." Chris reached for her, scooting his chair closer so they were inches apart. His blue-gray eyes were deep and serious. He wasn't trying to embarrass her. He honestly thought this was important. "Show me what you enjoy, what makes you feel good."

His palm cupped the back of her neck, his thumb stroking rhythmically over the pulse at her throat. The path he traced tingled and the beat beneath his touch thumped steadily faster.

"It will help if I know what excites you most, how to distract your mind if memories surface." His breath caressed her skin, his voice coaxing. "Show me." He reached for her hand and placed it palm up over her own breast.

The nipple hardened instantly, pebbling through the layers of bright pink silk and dark green cotton. Her body went liquid. As she watched, his eyes darkened to the color of smoke-hazed sky. Her lips parted.

And he let go. Standing, he took three steps away from the table and waited.

"What do you want me to do?" The words came out dry and painful. She wasn't sure about this but…

"Get comfortable. Why don't you get undressed and lie on the bed. I'll be there in a few minutes."

DARRELL STOOD in the shadows. The slam of the door of the neighboring cabin had startled him back into the night.

He'd walked around the cabin the friendly old biddy at the front desk had told him was his son's. No lights on inside meant either he was out or he was asleep. Ten o'clock wasn't Chris's usual bedtime so he'd guessed out.

He'd been about to try the front door when someone had stepped onto the front porch of the cabin thirty feet away. He really hoped whoever it was didn't plan to camp out because the mosquitoes were eating him alive.

He settled against the trunk of a tree to wait and nearly swore when Chris moved into the circle of the porch light.

That idiotic grandma couldn't tell her ass from an orangutan. She must have given him the wrong number. Fantastic.

His son walked to the railing, leaned over and appeared ready to stay there all night. *Shit.* Darrell fought the urge to slap the little monster sucking blood from the back of his calf. The last thing he needed was for Chris to discover he'd followed him up here.

Apparently, luck was on his side though, because just a few minutes after Chris came out, to gaze broodingly down into the grass in front of the porch, he checked his watch and went back inside.

With a loud crack, Darrell murdered the mosquito at his neck and headed back to the car he'd parked several cabins down. Now that he knew which cabin was Chris's, he'd wait. And watch.

On the drive up here, fueled with the boy's food and Scotch, he'd come to a decision. This was no longer just about getting money. This was about teaching his disrespectful son a lesson he should have learned a long time ago.

He was the boy's father. And he'd given his son an order. After looking at the casual opulence that filled Chris's home, it was obvious the boy had more than enough to give him the money he'd asked for.

Grown or not, his son needed to learn the meaning of respect. And he was man enough to teach that lesson.

9

KARYN WALKED into the bedroom, stood just inside the doorway and stared down at the huge bed.

An unexpected buzz of excitement raced down her spine. Was she going to do this or not? If she was, it was time to commit. No more looking back. No more second-guessing.

Part of her wished she could talk to Anne. Her friend would remind her of all the reasons this was good—and probably come up with a brilliant way to get over the embarrassment and kill the butterflies. She didn't have time to make a phone call, though. Chris would be in here in a minute; she'd heard the screen door bang shut behind him. Besides, this was something she needed to decide on her own. It was put up or shut up.

Grasping the hem of her sweater, she ran the edge through her fingers, took a deep breath and jerked it off over her head. Her jeans followed as she pushed them over her hips. She'd made the motions millions of times before; they were a habit she never thought of. But as her eyes caught her half-naked body in the mirror, she paused.

She liked the hot-pink color against her pale skin. It was bright and shocking. And gave her a blast of courage. Any woman wearing these panties should be bold, fearless, adventurous. A tingle shot through her body to settle between her thighs. She let her hand rest against her stomach, at first to quell the flutter there, but then because the sensation felt so good.

She watched her reflection as her hands traveled up to touch her silk-covered breasts. She could see him there, in her mind, standing behind her, watching the same image with those smoke-and-sky eyes. Suddenly the thought of pleasuring herself while Chris watched tantalized instead of troubled.

And then he was there. She hadn't heard the door or his footsteps on the worn wooden floor. It didn't matter. What did was the way he stared, his face, his hands, his body drawn tight.

She licked her lips. "What should I do?"

Without taking his eyes from her reflection, he crossed to the bed, pulled back the covers and piled the pillows before holding out a hand to her across the stark white sheet.

"Whatever feels good."

He helped her climb onto the bed but instead of joining her like she'd hoped, he disappeared back into the other room, quickly returning with a kitchen chair. He placed it in the corner, as far away from the lonely bed as he could get and sat down.

Night had fully fallen and the stars hadn't quite come out. The corner he'd picked was almost completely shrouded in darkness, only a few strips of weak moonlight fighting through. She could see his eyes and the sharp planes of his face, half his arms and torso, but nothing below the waist. Nowhere near as clearly as he could see her.

"Why don't you lie down? Take your bra and panties off?" His voice melted down her spine. It was the same one she'd been listening to for months, Dr. Desire, deep, dark, decadent.

She did what he asked. Sitting up, she opened the clasp of her bra, held the cups to her body and let the straps fall from her arms. Her breasts felt heavy, swollen, the nipples thrusting tight and aching against her crossed arms.

She let them drop free, the release liberating in a way she hadn't expected.

His eyes traveled her body, making her stomach roll with anticipation and fear. Oh God. What if she couldn't do this?

"You're fine, Karyn. Now your panties." He must have read her mind. Or her eyes. She was certain the fear that had jolted through her had been plain to see. But he was right. She was fine.

With a deep, calming breath, she lay back against the pillows and pushed her panties over her hips. She was alone, the only person driving this show. She could stop at any time.

In that moment she understood why this had been so important to him. She was in control and would be every single moment of their first sexual connection.

Chris folded his arms across his chest, the muscles bulging against the short sleeves of his shirt. He looked so far away over there in the corner. She was naked. He was fully clothed. Something about this whole thing seemed voyeuristic and naughty.

She fought the urge to cover herself. "I feel silly."

"There's nothing to be embarrassed about."

"That's easy for you to say. You're not the one naked. You can see every part of me but I can barely make you out against the shadows."

He sighed. She heard the gentle sound more than saw the movement. He stood, grabbed his chair and moved it forward into a patch of light from the other room.

"Better?"

Yes and no. She could see him all right. Including the hard gleam in his eyes. Her pulse quickened at the intensity of his stare.

"I'd offer to undress, and I will if you really want me to, but I don't think that would be a good idea."

She gripped the sheet beneath her and shifted higher against the pillows.

"Why not?"

"Because I'm close enough to the edge already."

The spot between her thighs clenched and warmed. She knew he wanted her sexually, had seen the evidence for herself several times in the past few weeks, but somehow hearing him say the words was exactly what she needed.

She'd agreed to this. It seemed important to him. "Will you help me?"

"Yes. Anything."

"Tell me what to do. I need you to start me off."

"Push the covers to the floor so I can see you better."

She hesitated for just a moment before kicking out with her legs and shoving the heavy quilt away. It slithered off the bed, landing in a pile to the side, leaving her completely naked and vulnerable.

Heat flared in his dark blue eyes. An answering flame flickered deep inside her belly.

She'd done the right thing asking him to do this. The fact that he sat just feet away from her, denying himself when she was naked in front of him, told her everything she needed to know about the man.

"Cup your breasts in your hands." She did, following his direction, doing exactly what they both wanted. "Now roll your nipples between your fingers." Her back arched in response to the touch.

Her mind played tricks. She knew her own hands caressed her body. But so did his. It was his thumbs brushing roughly across her distended nipples, his palms stroking the heavy weight of her breasts.

She pinched, torturing herself and if his tightened jaw was any indication, torturing him. A zing of electricity shot to her sex. The feeling was familiar and yet different. She'd experienced the shocks and swirls of arousal, had pulled them from her own body many times. This time there was a sharper edge, a keener pleasure in the experience.

Her muscles tightened and her hips moved restlessly against the bed.

Shifting her hands down across her stomach, she let her fingers brush the seam of her tightly closed thighs before moving back up again. She did it repeatedly, enjoying the feel and the way Chris's eyes darkened to match the night outside. His eyelids lowered and his arms rippled with tension.

She was teasing them both, tantalizing herself and him with the touch she wanted most.

"Spread your legs. Let me see." His words were low and husky and made her sex even wetter. She writhed against the sheet that had twisted beneath her, trying to relieve some of the building pressure.

Shifting her legs apart, she let her hands fall between her barely opened thighs.

"Wider. Let me see what I can't touch. Please."

She licked her lips. His mouth parted, his own tongue unconsciously mimicking her trail of moisture. She wanted to feel the heat of his mouth against her skin, pressing kisses to her stomach, tickling the inside of her thighs. Her eyes were weighted with the need to close, to surrender herself to that fantasy. She fought against it. Nothing in her mind could compare to the sight of Chris watching her, wanting her.

Her body throbbed to the rhythm of his speeding breath. She wanted his caress. Knew he wanted it, too. But he wouldn't give it. He'd decided, for some insane reason, that she needed this experience to ease her into sex. What he didn't understand, and apparently she couldn't explain, was that right now, all she wanted was him.

His gaze traveled up and down her body. She let her hands travel the same path his eyes did, touching every place he lingered. Until everything settled at the apex of her thighs where a sharp pleasure that bordered on pain pulsed.

"Show me." He leaned forward in the chair, his body straining closer to hers.

She slipped her fingers into the folds, her lungs caving with the pleasure as she rubbed across the nub of nerves hidden inside.

"Are you wet?"

Her own arousal surged across her fingers. She spread herself open to show him. "Yes."

Chris shifted on the chair, drawing her attention to the unmistakable ridge of his erection. He was there, right at the end of her bed. So close and yet not nearly close enough.

"Please come over here." She heard the begging edge to her words and tried to hate herself for the weakness, but couldn't, not while she was burning hot with the need for him.

"I can't. I want to, but I can't. Show me, Karyn. I want to watch while you let go."

A breeze shifted across her body, touching her exposed core and making the muscles contract. She wanted his touch, but if he wouldn't give it to her...

She slipped a single finger inside. Her moisture coated her hand and her eyes slid shut as she sank into the dampness. She could feel every flutter of her inner muscles. Her breath caught in her throat as she moved, pulling in and out with deliberate strokes. It felt so good, but even as her mind fogged with the visceral response of her body she knew there was more, knew that if Chris had been with her the experience would have been so much better.

Her thumb rolled back and forth against her clit. Her fingers pumped faster and faster against her sex. Her muscles pulled tight and her hips strained for a deeper touch.

Her breath panted out between parted lips. Her teeth sank into the swollen flesh of her bottom lip, but she barely registered the twinge of pain.

"Look at me."

Chris's words somehow slipped through. And she obeyed. Her eyes opened, moving unerringly to his. She saw him, the sharp stamp of arousal on his face registering somewhere in the back of her mind.

She wanted to speak, to ask him to finish this for her, but she couldn't. Not around the keening groan that erupted from her lungs as she exploded in a climax that was much more powerful than any she'd experienced before.

Her eyelids flickered as wave after wave shook through her body. When it finally stopped, she sank into the mattress in a pile of spent muscle and bone. She couldn't form a coherent thought. She simply concentrated on breathing, not entirely sure her brain could have kept the necessary function going without conscious effort.

Chris was there; she had heard the creak of the chair, but couldn't open her eyes to look. A few minutes. That was all she needed.

He didn't give them to her. Leaning over the bed, he pressed a lingering kiss to her forehead. His breath washed across her skin, labored, almost painful sounding in its intensity. The sheet beneath her bunched with the pull of his fists at her side. Even through her sex-clouded brain she could feel the coiled tension whipping through his body. Her own humming nerve endings responded to the electrical charge of his desire.

She wanted to reach for him, but none of her muscles responded. Before she could muster the strength to make them, he said, "Thank you. I'll see you tomorrow," in a hoarse whisper and disappeared.

Reality slowly returned. Sanity, clarity, a bit of embarrassment at what she'd done. And so did the ache, the incessant ache that had been her constant companion since the night they'd first met.

Karyn rolled from the bed, standing naked in the middle of

the room, alone. She stared out the window into the clear night sky. This was Saturday night. They'd leave sometime tomorrow.

She'd started this weekend knowing that by the end of it she would be whole again. That she'd come home with that last step taken, ready to move on with the life she'd always wanted.

While the last hour had been the most erotic of her life, Chris seriously needed to pick up the pace or that wouldn't happen.

Moving over, she placed her palm against the cool, air-conditioned glass. There would be no shopping tomorrow. No fun, no games, no more steps.

At least not his. She had a few of her own. Starting nice and early. There was no more time to waste.

DARRELL FOUND a bar in town, enjoyed a couple of drinks, a game of pool and the chance to use a bathroom that didn't smell like pine trees and decaying leaves.

Killing time was something he'd gotten very good at over the years. He could relax with the best of them, though his tastes usually were a little finer than what roadside bars offered. But beggars couldn't be choosers.

"Last call. You want another?"

Darrell swallowed the last dregs of his beer, glanced at his watch and declined. It was almost two o'clock, surely even his son would be asleep by now.

Parking at the other end of the row of cabins this time, Darrell once more crept through the shadows to Chris's. He watched for several minutes, trying to spot even the faintest flicker of light or motion. Nothing.

With careful steps, he inched up the porch, cringing each time one of the ancient boards let out a screech. He turned the front knob, expecting the door to be locked—but it didn't hurt to try. When it was, he moved to the flanking windows.

The problem with staying in a quaint little Southern town was that people tended to forget the world wasn't quaint or safe.

The third one he tried opened about half an inch. With a little elbow grease and some curse words at a squeak, the thing gave way enough to let him through.

Sneaking quietly into what appeared to be a sitting area, he glanced around the small, combined space, noting the immaculate kitchen and a table with half-melted candles. On the floor sat a woman's handbag.

So his son had been romancing someone. A spurt of fatherly pride rushed in. Moving carefully, Darrell dug through the bag and removed a wallet. Flipping it open, he strained to see the driver's license. Karyn Mitchell. And a Birmingham address. But in the moonlight, her photo was just a dark silhouette. Darrell debated taking the credit cards and small amount of money before dropping the wallet back in the bag. Best to play it safe until his greedy brat coughed up his cash.

A sigh echoed from an open door. He crept closer to see inside. A high, four-poster bed dominated the space. But where he'd expected to find two bodies, he only found one. And there was no mistaking for his son the woman curled beneath the covers.

Where was Chris?

Darrell took a quick, calculating look around. The cabin was small. From his vantage point in the bedroom doorway he could see into both the bathroom and the living space. No one was there.

Chris was not in the cabin. Of that he was certain.

Walking with quiet steps, Darrell peered at the woman and nearly jerked back. It was the same one from the picture, the same one he'd seen Chris devouring in the parking lot days ago.

So his son had brought this woman on his weekend getaway. And he obviously wasn't sleeping in her bed.

What an idiot.

She shifted in her sleep with a sound somewhere between a sigh and a whimpering groan before rolling to her other side. The covers slipped down, leaving her back completely bare to the crease of her ass.

She was naked. And her skin glowed in the moonlight. Her long hair, dark red in this light, spread out against her back and the stark white sheet beneath her.

His erection was instant. He reached for her, moving his hand down the curve of her inviting spine without actually touching.

His knuckles brushed at the edge of sheet, hoping the small touch might dislodge it and give him a hint of her breasts. He could see their outline, full and firm, but he wanted more. It had been so long since he'd felt a woman.

He wasn't sure what woke her, but one moment he was staring at the soft play of light across her skin, the next she was screaming down the place.

He bolted, certain he'd left his heart seizing in fright somewhere on her floor.

10

KARYN'S SCREAMS jarred Chris wide awake. He was out of his cabin and halfway to hers before the echo had even died.

Barefoot and naked except for the pajama bottoms he'd thrown on, he wasted precious seconds fumbling with the extra key to her door. He was in and at her side within minutes.

"What's wrong? What happened?"

Karyn stood in the center of the living room, the sheet clutched tightly to her body with hands that were far from steady. At least she wasn't screaming, not anymore.

"I'm fine."

Her voice was strong, but the smile she tried to give him trembled before she gave up on the effort.

"No, you're not. What happened?"

"I was having a dream." Her skin flushed hot as she tucked the sheet tighter beneath her arms. He wasn't sure if the stain of color was from embarrassment or adrenaline. "I woke up and thought someone was in the room, touching me."

She glanced around at the empty place. "But no one was here."

"Are you sure?"

"Yes. The place is small. There's no one here." He watched her pull that plump lower lip into her mouth and gently bite down on the abundant flesh.

She didn't hold it long.

"I was dreaming of you."

He liked the sound of that, especially since he'd been pulled from a dream of his own where he'd had his hands all over her. But her white-knuckled grip on the sheet and the fear in her eyes quickly banished his satisfaction. Her dream may have started with a fantasy, but it had apparently turned to a nightmare.

Chris wanted to kick himself. Why had he left her alone tonight? Why hadn't he considered that while she might not show any outward effects from her first sexual encounter in years, in sleep she could be vulnerable to subconscious fears?

Reaching for her, he wrapped her in his arms and rubbed his palms up and down her back. When her body stopped its tiny tremors, he led her over to the couch and urged her down with him, pulling her into his lap.

Burying himself in a corner, he cradled her body with his own, her sheet-covered back to his naked chest. They sat in silence for a while, the normal night sounds wrapping around them. He enjoyed the feel of her. The simplicity of having his arms around her, her body relaxed trustingly against his own. It was…nice.

And even though the primal urge to take her throbbed quietly beneath his skin, for now he could ignore it.

"Was it him, the man who raped you, in your dream?"

Her body stiffened against his, but she didn't move away and after a few moments she relaxed once more, one muscle at a time.

"No. It wasn't him. Although, I have to admit, once I was out of bed and my head cleared a bit, it did cross my mind. The rape."

He let the words hang, unwilling to ask more questions. If she wanted to tell him, fine. If not, well that was the rule he'd agreed to.

With a sigh, she snuggled deeper against him. "You know, I honestly don't think about it very often. I'm not saying the memories don't surface because they do, every once in a while. Not nearly as much as they used to, though.

"I think maybe it's kinda like death, just the death of your trust in people, in yourself. Time passes and you realize that eventually life goes on even without that part of yourself."

He knew exactly what she was talking about.

"I felt that way when my mother died, like nothing else in the world would ever matter again. But it did. I was too busy trying to survive, to deal with supporting myself and saving money for college to wallow. Years later I looked up and realized it didn't hurt as much anymore."

"Exactly. The trial was like limbo, years of my life where things would be fine for months and suddenly some lawyer would need me for deposition or trial practice or the judge would rule on some motion and half the papers in the state would run a story about me and my life."

"Why?"

Karyn leaned her head back and looked up into his face. "He was a starter for the MSU football team, a junior with one more year of eligibility that the school and fans didn't want to lose. I, on the other hand, thought he should rot in jail for a while."

She shrugged and shifted back around. "He won. On both accounts. One of the alums posted his bail, and the trial conveniently didn't interfere with his season. And then, of course, the jury found him not guilty after the defense pulled the teenage years of my life through the mud.

"You know, I think that was the worst part of it. The emotional scars from the rape started to heal long before the ones from the way they ripped apart my life. All those salacious stories about when I lost my virginity with my boyfriend at sixteen, the frat boy I'd met on a trip to visit Blake my senior year. They made it sound like I was the Mississippi State slut.

There must have been five or six men step forward and swear I'd had sex with them. The truth was two."

She twisted against him and he could feel her anger in her body.

"That was hard, knowing people read those stories. And believed them. My friends. Neighbors. Parents. At one point my mother told me to drop the charges. She begged me not to put the family through any more. As if their embarrassment meant more than what I'd gone through. Meant more than making sure this man could never hurt anyone again.

"Nothing in my life was private or safe. Nothing. Not after that night."

The words stopped. She closed her mouth and rolled her head to stare at the ceiling.

With his arms wrapped tightly around her, Chris fought hard to keep his muscles from tensing with the unadulterated desire to beat the living shit out of someone—preferably the coward who'd raped her.

He'd been angry when he'd heard her story that night. Hell, half the city had been. But now it was personal. He wanted the retribution she'd been denied.

But he obviously wouldn't get it. And right now Karyn needed him, so he simply held her and waited.

It took several minutes, but slowly the rigidity eased from her muscles again. Her legs stirred beneath the swaddled sheet pooled around her body.

Her heat burned through the cotton sheet to his naked skin. He'd thought the barrier enough, along with her story and the nightmare, to keep his desire contained. It wasn't. In fact, the thin sheet made it worse.

He'd seen the body beneath, knew the curve of her breasts and the soft pink color of her sex, how it darkened the more she became aroused.

She shifted back in his lap, grinding the cleft of her buttocks into his erection. He knew she recognized his response from the way she melted against him and pressed harder.

He needed to get up. Get out of there. Before he did something wrong. There was no way they could have sex right now. She'd just spilled her guts to him after a nightmare had reminded her of her rape. Because of a sexual encounter that he'd talked her into.

She wasn't ready.

This wasn't the right time.

"I need you, Chris. Please. Help me take this last step. Help me forget."

KARYN'S HEART POUNDED in her ears. She thought for sure Chris could hear it. But that didn't matter. Nothing did except for getting him naked and inside her.

Yes, she was scared. But with Chris, need far outweighed the fear. Earlier she'd needed him to comfort and listen. And he had. Now she needed him to take her. And he would…

If she had anything to say about it.

Turning to face him, she pushed up from the couch, trailing her hands down his body as she wriggled herself out of the warm cocoon he had provided. The sheet slid down her skin and into a heap on the floor. She was naked; the only thing touching her was air and a single ray of moonlight.

Chris swallowed. She watched the strong column of his throat work and enjoyed the surge of feminine power that washed through her. "I don't think this is a good idea, Karyn. There are a few more things we should do first, like—"

"Nothing else, Chris. Nothing but your hands on my body, your mouth on my skin, you deep inside me, will do right now."

She reached for him, taking his hand and lacing their fingers together. She couldn't pull him off the couch, not if he didn't want to come with her. The hard, thick ridge in his lap gave her the courage to be bold.

"How many times have you admonished callers for not listening to their partners?"

He eyed her warily, but answered anyway. "Frequently."

"Then perhaps you should take your own advice, Dr. Desire, and listen to me. I'm ready. I trust you. I want this. I want you. Preferably right now."

"You just had a nightmare about the rape. Now is not—"

"Now is the perfect time *because* of the nightmare. I'm tired of letting the fear control me, my life, my choices. Help me break free."

Chris looked at her. Not just at her body, her breasts, her sex, but the woman she was beneath. She could tell the difference.

In his eyes she saw emotions gathering, like a summer storm. She couldn't read him, though, had no idea what he would do. Until he stood, bringing their joined hands to rest at the curve of her nape.

"If you're sure."

"Absolutely." Those butterflies lifted off as soon as she said the word. She knew she would be fine.

He touched his lips to hers in a kiss that held absolutely no demand. Her own hand fell limp to her side as he let go and began massaging the back of her neck. It was delicious, the taste of his mouth and the magic of his hand against her tensed muscles.

Yes. Now. It would be fine, now.

Karyn opened to him and took what she wanted, tugging the kiss deeper, nipping at his lip and curling her fingers into his hair-roughened chest.

She took the kiss from slow and smoldering to frenzied in about three seconds.

And he stopped it. Pulling back, he breathed, "Slow down," against her lips. "We have hours to do this right."

He worked her hands from his chest and held them with his own. His fingers rubbed the insides of her wrists, sending sparks through her arms. She recognized the motion as something meant to soothe and reassure her. Like the gentle rubbing of a dog's fur to distract him from the shot of medication he was about to get.

This experience might be medicinal, but she wanted no anesthetic. She wanted to experience every moment. She just wanted them over quickly, like pulling off a Band-Aid with one jerk.

"You might have hours, but I've waited years for this. We can do slow later."

"Years, huh? I distinctly remember you writhing under the power of an orgasm not four hours ago."

"And I distinctly remember you walking out the door while I was still catatonic, with no more than a kiss on my forehead."

"You weren't complaining then."

"I'm complaining now. Touch me."

She looked up into his face, passive, relaxed, controlled. But something dark and primitive filled his blue-gray eyes. A ribbon of white-hot need melted through her body.

He shifted, the slightest bunching of muscles, and suddenly the flimsy layer of confidence she'd hidden behind disappeared and the edge of anxiety sharpened. She pushed it away. She wanted this. More than she'd wanted anything else for the past several years. More even than she'd wanted justice.

"Are you scared, Karyn?"

"Not anymore."

"Good. But I need you to be honest with me. Promise me. I'll stop anytime, just ask."

She nodded, licking her lips and testing the hold he had on her hands. She wanted to touch him, like in the parking lot of her office building. Only, this time she wouldn't just feel the cotton covering his skin, she'd feel his flesh and bone, hair and heat. Her stomach tightened and her thighs clenched.

"There's only what works for you and me." He moved closer, snugging his mouth up to the sensitive spot just behind her ear and taking a testing nip. "You're not the only one strung tight, Karyn. I've been fantasizing about finding those secret spots that make your breath catch for days. You had an orgasm earlier tonight. I could only watch. And want."

"Mmm," was about all she could manage with his tongue licking a moist trail across her neck. "I like that. Do it again."

"I can't."

She jerked back, staring up at him in surprise. "Why not?"

He didn't answer, simply took her hand and led her back to the couch. She sat gingerly when he urged her down, but curled her hands into the sofa cushions and gathered her legs beneath her, ready to spring. "Wait. I want—"

His hands wrapped around her shoulders, their weight holding her still when all she wanted was to get up, to walk to the bedroom, to experience sex for the first time in years.

"I know what you want. What excites you. Trust me."

His hands slipped from her shoulders, tickling down the sides of her neck. He picked the sheet up off the floor and draped it across her body before disappearing from view.

If he'd been any other man she would have moved her head, would have followed where he went, what he was doing. But she didn't. Instead, she concentrated on each breath flowing through her body.

She didn't need to see him to know where he was. She could hear him, smell him, sense his presence behind her.

His hands settled on her shoulders again. His thumbs dug into the knot at the base of her neck, his fingers massaged the curved muscles, rolling her head and loosening the tension there.

Her eyes closed as a wave of contented bliss washed through her. *Relaxation.* She let her head fall back against the sofa as his talented hands moved down over her arms. That's something she hadn't expected to feel. Something she hadn't known she needed.

If he made her feel this way just by touching her shoulders and neck, she couldn't imagine what he would do to the places that mattered most.

He towered over her, so tall and male. She had a brief flashback to their first dinner together. That night she'd thought the same thing. So much had changed in such a short space of time. Not to the world outside, but in her. And him.

The tension came back with a bang. *Stop. Don't you do it. Don't you dare fall for him.* Her mind buzzed a warning his hands convinced her to ignore.

Her heart was in no danger. She'd only known him a couple of weeks, not nearly long enough to fall in love. This was a fling. And after it ended—and it would, because Dr. Desire didn't do permanent—her life would start brand-new.

They'd share chemistry and hopefully good sex. Nothing more.

His fingers flexed against her skin. She leaned her head back, opened her heavy-lidded eyes and stared up into his face. Shadows played as he moved back and forth with each massaging motion, highlighting the arch of his brow bone, the sharp line of his nose and his lips, pulled straight into an expression of sensual concentration.

He looked like a man trying to find the solution to world peace, not someone looking forward to hours of pleasure. Until his eyes met hers. There. Everything she'd wanted to see and more. Heat. Promise. Desire.

She wanted him to enjoy this experience as much as she did. She didn't need controlled determination from him. She might not have as much practice as he did when it came to sex, but even she knew that loosening up would lead to a much more fulfilling experience for them both.

She took a breath, her back arching up off the sofa, and let the sheet slip from her breasts. It was a silent invitation for more, one she hoped he couldn't ignore. She reached for him, speared her hands into his hair, tugging until he curled toward her.

His lips parted and his mouth touched hers. She opened for him. The angle of his body changed the experience of the kiss, sparking something deep inside.

His hand nudged the underside of her jaw, guiding her up off the sofa and even closer to him. His fingers left an imprint in her skin. She could feel the distinct length of each one, not from the force of his hold, but from the burn of his touch.

His teeth latched on to her bottom lip, sucking it into his mouth. He bit down, a prick of momentary pain before his tongue smoothed over her smarting flesh. Moisture gathered between her legs. She shifted, trying to relieve the ache.

Nothing helped.

She tore her mouth away. "As much as I'm enjoying this, you don't have to do it."

"Do what?"

"This whole seduction scene. I'm a sure thing."

His hand brushed her forehead, sweeping a strand of hair away. "Who said this was for you?"

With a single finger, he skimmed the curve of her neck, the arc of her shoulder, the hollow of her collarbone. Her nipples tightened with a stinging ache as that lonely caress drew closer. He skirted the swell at the side of her breast, making her breath catch, down the crease of arm and rib to push the sheet farther from her body.

The air-conditioning kicked on. A puff of air swept across her exposed skin making her abdomen dance. Chris picked up her hand with his and placed it right where the muscles had clenched.

Tugging her hand against his hold, she tried to break away,

to feel the whole of his palm on her skin without the buffer of her own. But he wouldn't budge, would not let her free.

Instead he pulled both their hands up her body. It was the path she'd traveled just hours before while he watched. This time she wanted something different, something more.

"Chris, I…"

Her voice trailed off as their joined hands settled over one breast, and the breath left her body. For the first time she experienced the full force of his touch against her skin as his fingers flowed over one nipple and then to the other. With a fingernail, he stopped to flick them and she jerked forward for more.

Instead he moved away and she whimpered.

She was like a piece of the melted candle across the room, liquid and warm, certain that without the containment of her skin she'd spill everywhere and puddle at his feet.

She watched the wheels spin in his uneasy blue eyes. Protests formed, reasoned, fought against need. He was going to try to stall, because he thought it was the right thing to do for her.

If she'd ever had a twinge of doubt that Chris was the right man for this, it would have evaporated in that one moment.

She could smell his arousal, the heady scent mixing with her own. If she turned her head, she would see the unmistakable ridge of his penis, long, hard, thick. This man wanted her. And yet he would deny them both because he thought it was the right thing to do.

Staring up into his face, she dropped every ounce of self-preservation and pretense. All that was left was an intense hunger. If she was being honest, that was what she feared most, that after tonight she'd never experience that burning pleasure again. But…having it once was better than never experiencing the joy at all.

"I need you. Take me to bed."

_11_

CHRIS COULDN'T FIGHT her anymore. Couldn't ignore the desire flooding every square inch of his being. At this precise moment, he couldn't even remember why it had been so all-fired important to wait to touch her pale, smooth skin.

Unable to stop himself, he reached for her, trailing a single finger down the curve of her neck to the slope of her shoulder. She shuddered.

The sensation exhilarated and pushed him even closer to the edge. He'd been denying them both for far too long.

He gave in to the yearning to taste her, burying his hands in her hair and pulling her close. Their mouths touched and he knew it was over. He'd never get enough of the sensation, not just of her touch, taste and scent, but of the way being next to her made him feel. Alive. Strong. Male.

The first contact of her body against his blew the breath right from his lungs. His hands stroked up and down the curve of her back, enjoying the way she shivered. Filling his palms with the sweet curve of her ass, he pulled her tighter to his body.

His fingers slipped into the crevice there, finding her wet and hot. God, he wanted so much more. But not yet.

She moaned when he pulled away, ground her hips against him, looking for relief. Plunging her own hands past the waistband of his pajama pants, she reached for him. His erection jerked toward the touch he wanted so desperately, but he caught her hands and pulled them away before they found their mark.

"This first time we're concentrating on you."

He reached for her, intent on sweeping her into his arms and carrying her to the bed for better access to everything she offered.

Taking a step back she said, "No."

"What?"

"No. This first time is not going to be about me. It's not going to be special. It's going to be unbridled, down-and-dirty sex, right here on the floor."

There was no doubt he looked dumbfounded. He certainly felt like he'd fallen through a rabbit hole somewhere.

"You're crazy. There's a perfectly good bed five steps away."

"And I don't want anything to do with it. I don't want you concentrating on what should come next or whether I'm fighting back memories."

She laid a hand at the center of his chest. Her fingertips brushed so close to his heart he was sure she could feel every frenetic beat. "The only thing I want either of us to think about is pleasure and how we can get more."

Dark-red hair clouded around her face. All he could see were her eyes, full of heat—and hope.

He'd seen hope before. It had once filled his mother's eyes. The worst moment of his life had been watching it fade to despair, then desolation, then to nothing.

The thought of watching it disappear from Karyn froze the blood in his veins and constricted his chest.

He'd never met another person who had experienced so much pain and still managed to embrace life. He certainly didn't—not as much as he should. What she viewed as a personal defect in herself, he saw as intelligent self-protection.

"Trust me, Chris. I'm fine. And I want this more than you'll

ever know. Make love to me. Fully. Completely. With everything you have inside."

She let her hand trail down his body, dipping and swirling,
touching and teasing with every word. When it finally slipped
beneath the waistband of his pants, his body turned to stone
beneath her touch. Living, breathing, begging rock.

"I'm just trying—"

"I know. And I appreciate the sentiment, but that's not
what I need."

Staring down into her, he saw the truth looking back at him.
He grabbed her, pulling her up off her feet, and crushed her to
him, unable to fight anymore.

KARYN'S HEAD WENT LIGHT. Not from the surprising loss of
floor, but from the giddy realization of what she'd done. She
hadn't thought it possible to become more aroused than she
already was. She'd been wrong.

Wrapping her legs around his waist, she clung to him. His
sex throbbed; she could feel every pulse jammed tight against
her own. The fabric between them was already wet, whether
from him or her it didn't matter.

Chris grabbed a blanket from the back of the couch, flung
it onto the floor beneath them and stretched them both out on
top. It wasn't much padding for the hard wood beneath. Karyn
didn't care.

His mouth latched tight over one of her nipples, sucking
hard before laving the tightened nub with his tongue. A string
seemed to snap between his mouth and her sex, pulling her hips
up off the floor in a search for more.

He didn't disappoint. His hand was there, slipping through
the folds, rubbing her clit and sliding home. While everywhere
else his mouth and hands were so fierce they bordered on
bruising, here he was gentle, deliberate, soft.

But she wanted fierce. She wanted abandon. She wanted passion to blind them both.

Rearing up, she tore at his pants, pulling them ruthlessly down as far as she could push them.

"Take them off." Her voice was deep and breathless, almost unrecognizable to her own ears.

But he did as she asked, leaving her momentarily bereft. She looked up at him from the floor, her chest heaving as if she'd run a marathon.

She enjoyed the view as a single strip of silver shining through the window cut from his shoulder to the tip of his hip bone jutting out over the gray cotton. She should have felt open, exposed, sitting there on the ground, naked, at his feet. But she didn't. She couldn't. Not when he was staring at her, his eyes heavy-lidded with sexual promise.

Then the pants disappeared and only one thing held her attention—his erection.

It sprang free, long, hard and inviting. She wanted to touch, couldn't stop herself from licking her lips at the thought of feeling that hot flesh against her own tongue.

But he wouldn't let her. Before she could scoot forward an inch he was beside her again. His arms wrapped tightly around her, gently lowering her back down to the floor.

Before she could do anything about it, he shifted, covering her sex with his palm and dipping his fingers slowly back inside.

She squirmed at the touch, wanting more.

He obliged. Stroking harder, longer, faster. Her hips pumped, finding a maddening rhythm that drove her higher and higher.

Her body tightened, gathered strength. His mouth touched down squarely on hers, his tongue requesting entrance. One single stroke inside, mirrored by the tantalizing touch of his fingers deep at her core and she exploded.

The sensation was like nothing and everything she'd ever experienced. The same and yet absolutely different.

It took her several minutes for reality to set back in, for the world around her to right itself and register. Chris lay beside her, propped on an elbow staring down at her with eyes sharp and focused. A flutter started again deep in her belly.

"How are you?" His voice was sandpaper gruff.

She licked her lips, needing the moisture. "Hmm…I could be better."

He didn't protest as she pushed against his shoulder, tipping him onto his back at the border of the blanket.

The worst of her desire had been sated, the sharp edge now gone. But she knew it would build quickly again, stoked higher by the realization that what she'd experienced had only been a taste.

She felt free. With him. Free to explore and embrace a side of herself she'd denied for far too long.

Giddy with the excitement and power, she leaned down into his body, trailing kisses down his chest and ribs. She enjoyed the stuttered stop of his breath whenever she touched a sensitive spot. The way his stomach muscles strained tight as her fingers tickled across the skin there.

A tiny pearl of moisture leaked from the tip of his penis, shining brightly in the darkness. She wanted to lick it, to taste him, to discover whether he was sweet or salty, smooth and powerful.

His hand clamped around her shoulder, trying to reverse their positions.

She looked up into his smoldering eyes and felt an answering fire burn brighter inside. "Let me."

"No. Let me." With a suddenness that knocked speech from her brain, he flipped their positions so that she lay once again on her back and he knelt at her side.

Openmouthed kisses traced down her inner thighs, tickling and teasing a path of destruction. He bent her knees up and pulled her wide open, exposing her to anything he wished to do. His breath kissed her skin just before his tongue laved her clit.

She bucked at the sensation, wanting more. He tortured her senseless, driving every thought but the need he created from her mind.

One thought struggled through, as she moved closer and closer to another orgasm, another one alone. This was not what she wanted.

Grabbing his head, she jerked hard, knowing if she didn't get his attention now in another minute it would be too late. "Stop," panted out between broken breaths.

He immediately backed away—which was both good and bad.

"No, Chris. I want you inside me. Please."

He stared down at her, and for a brief moment she was afraid he might refuse.

"Condom?" The single word burst from his lips.

"Top drawer by the bed."

With a haste she applauded, he disappeared for a few moments before quickly returning with several pale-blue packets he dropped to the floor.

"You are so beautiful. I can't deny you anything."

His eyes staring deep into her own, he slipped inside, filling her more than she'd ever thought possible. Something had been taken from her that night so long ago—not a piece of her soul, but a piece of her femininity, her sensuality. Her trust in the sexual side of her being. She'd suppressed it, denied it. Tonight Chris was giving it back.

He waited for several moments, for protest, panic, fear, she wasn't sure. It didn't matter. She allowed him that peace of mind.

They were centimeters apart, his blue eyes full of swirling

gray and green, with an edge of anxiety she should have been the one to feel. But she didn't. Not now.

Her chest ached, right at the center of her heart. Chris had stepped out of his element, out of himself, to do this for her.

She owed him so much.

He began to move, slowly at first, deliberate strokes that touched a sweet spot deep inside. She was so close, driven by him and the flood of desire she'd held back for so long.

Her body pulled tight as ripples started deep inside, small at first, but quickly growing larger and larger. They consumed her, taking over, body, mind and soul. A keening cry exploded from her lips—joined almost immediately by a growl of pleasure from Chris.

A single tear rolled down her cheek and into her hair. Not a tear of sadness, but of joy.

Through the pulsing convulsions and the contracting muscles, Karyn registered one thing that amazed her: Chris murmuring words in her ear. Not words of love, but of safety and comfort. "No one will ever hurt you again. I swear. No one…"

She hadn't needed them, but he'd offered them in case she had.

"Sonofabitch."

What had he done?

Precisely what he'd feared he would do—let his dick take over instead of listening to his head. And Karyn had been the one to pay the price for his lapse in control.

His body flushed hot then cold at the memory of that single tear rolling from the corner of her eye. He wanted to hurt someone, but he feared the asshole who deserved a beating was himself.

Chris breathed out and stared into the bedroom he'd just carried Karyn into. She'd murmured and smiled before rolling onto her side and drifting back to sleep. She looked so peaceful.

So why did he feel like hell?

Chris made a circuit of the cabin, rubbing at a tight spot in the center of his chest. Prowling through the living area, he checked the front windows, the door, the breakfast nook, more for something to do than anything else.

But surprise filled him when he reached the far wall. The last window sat half an inch open.

It hadn't been, earlier tonight. He knew because before he'd left her alone, he'd checked them all. He'd felt it his responsibility.

He stared at the open space, his mind moving a mile a minute. It hadn't been her imagination.

Several hours had passed since Karyn had screamed. Plenty of time for whoever had broken in to disappear. Chris jerked up the window, stuck his head out and looked around anyway.

No one.

Damn it! He slammed the window back down with a resounding bang. While he'd been losing his head, skipping several important steps and making love to Karyn, the man who'd scared the hell out of her had been getting away. He'd honestly thought it had been her imagination. But he should have checked just in case.

Now the man, whoever he was, was long gone.

Chris furiously flipped the lock on the window shut. A hollow feeling echoed through his stomach when he didn't hear a telltale click like the other windows had made.

He hadn't noticed it last night, but then he'd been a little preoccupied. He'd turned the lock and assumed it had caught like all the others.

A man had been inside Karyn's bedroom staring at her while she slept, reaching for her in the dark. Chris's mind flashed to the memory of her standing before him, the white sheet puddling at her feet.

And wanted to double over with the guilt. He'd hadn't protected her.

She'd been alone and vulnerable and he'd let a madman inside. And she had come to him for help and instead he'd left her crying.

He turned his back to the window and looked through the open doorway into Karyn's bedroom. Moonlight, so pure it was white-blue, fell across the foot of the bed. He could see her, standing there, one hand wrapped tightly around a post, staring back at him.

Her face, peaceful in the glowing darkness, held none of the fear he knew it would in a few moments.

She was breathtaking. And he was about to shatter that tranquility. But he had to tell her. She needed to know.

He crossed to her. The urge to reach for her was there, in fact, he couldn't remember wanting anything more. But he didn't. He had no idea what her reaction would be.

"Karyn—"

"I thought you had gone." The words were not an accusation, but rather a simple statement that heaped one more log of guilt to the already flaming fire.

"No." But she might wish he had. "It wasn't a nightmare."

"What wasn't?" She licked her lips, her gaze roaming from his face, across his chest and down.

"A side window was open. The man was real. He was inside."

Her eyes jerked up. A host of emotions flew across her face before settling on anger.

"I'm so sorry, Karyn—"

"Damn it. I attract them like flies."

He didn't expect that it would help but… "I don't think he was after you." If he'd had rape in mind, the intruder would have still been here when he'd run inside. "But we do need to call the police."

"What for? Is something missing?"

"No, but…"

"Look, I really don't want to deal with that tonight. They can't do anything. He didn't steal anything or hurt me."

"He broke into a rental cabin. What if this isn't the first time? We should report it."

"Tomorrow. Right now I want to go back to bed." She looped her arms around his neck and leaned into him. The cold shock of her skin had him sucking in a breath. Her nipples tightened and scraped through the hair on his chest to the skin beneath.

He should have pulled back, put space between them. But he didn't.

"We'll go to my cabin. I'll sleep on the couch."

"No. You won't."

His blood churned, thick and molten. He tried to ignore it, but he couldn't stop himself from reaching for her, from wrapping a hand beneath the long length of her hair and holding on so she wouldn't disappear.

"I saw the tear, Karyn. We moved too fast. You aren't ready for this."

"That had nothing to do with the past and everything to do with you." Moving closer, she brought their mouths together, infusing the connection with longing and joy. "I was happy, Chris, not sad or scared."

He stared down at her, the knot in his chest turning and writhing into a raw ache that scared him spitless. He cared. He cared too much.

"I told you everything tonight." Her hand covered the ache, easing what she didn't even know was there. "More than I've shared with anyone. And in return you set me free. I don't regret a moment. Thank you."

He didn't know what to say.

12

HE SCOOPED HER into his arms and she squealed. Whatever she'd expected it hadn't been that. Her protests grew louder as he headed for the door of the cabin instead of the bed.

"Where are you going? Put me down!"

"To my cabin. We're not staying here."

"I'm naked."

"And it's two in the morning. No one's outsi—"

His voice trailed off and his brows slammed together in a frown. Spinning on his heel, he headed back in the direction they'd just come, deposited her gently to the floor and said, "Grab what you need. We'll get the rest in the morning."

She quickly pulled on a turquoise negligee, simply because it was on top. He wouldn't even let her grab some shoes, again insisting on carrying her the few yards to his place.

At his cabin, she had a quick look around. The knickknacks and personal touches were different, but the general layout was the same. One big, open room and a bedroom toward the back.

Her focus zeroed in on the large four-poster bed.

Chris didn't disappoint her because that's exactly where he headed, laying her down on the fluffy surface and then joining her there.

But instead of reaching for her, he pulled the covers over them both, turned onto his side and wrapped his arm possessively around her waist.

Not what she wanted.

She wiggled out of his hold, turning to face him. "What are you doing?"

"Going to sleep."

"Um, no you're not."

A teasing smile played at the corners of his lips before he squashed it.

"Maybe you should take your own advice, Dr. Desire."

"What advice would that be?"

"Listening to your partner."

"Hmm…I don't hear you saying much."

Their first time together had been heavy with purpose. This time there was a lightness that also helped to heal her soul. This was for them both.

"Then you're not listening closely enough."

She threw a leg over his hips, straddling him. The slippery silk of her nightgown bunched around her thighs, but left the core of her body deliciously open. She settled her sex against his burgeoning erection, enjoying the feel of him close to her. He'd pulled his sleep pants back on earlier, and once again they were the only thing standing between her and unbelievable pleasure.

But she wasn't in a hurry, not this time. Now was for savoring.

One hand slid along his chest while the other reached between their bodies. She slipped her hand inside, filling her fist with as much of him as she could hold. Every smooth inch registered in her brain. She couldn't see what she held, but could close her eyes and remember.

Her fingers flexed slowly up his shaft, one heartbreaking squeeze at a time. She enjoyed the sensation, the exploration. The way his breath caught and held. She rocked against him, caressing a groan from his throat.

Her body moved in time to the caresses. She counted the

seconds with each throbbing pulse at the base of his neck. His hands wrapped around her hips, digging hard and pulling tight. The slippery fabric slid beneath his hold.

Bunching it in his hands, Chris skimmed it up her body. The chilled fabric and his hot grasp combined to send goose bumps raging across her skin.

His knuckles brushed the curve of her breasts, tantalizingly close to the pouting centers. He nudged the underside of her arms, asking her silently to let go. She did, but only for the second it took to pull the turquoise material over her head and throw it away.

Cool air touched her naked skin. The soft cotton between her legs abraded her thighs as she shifted against him. His muscles bunched; she enjoyed their coiled power. Right up until he surged forward, knocking her backward onto the bed. Air whooshed out of her lungs at the impact of his hard body settling over hers. The sensation startled her and alarmed her a little. But then her body went soft beneath his, sinking into the mattress with a melting sigh of pleasure.

His mouth traveled her body, leaving a moist trail of fire wherever he touched. They lay diagonally across the foot of the bed. Her feet hung off. It didn't matter. What did was the mind-numbing assault he waged against her lips. His hands massaged her breasts, stroked her stomach, dipped down into the slippery cleft of her sex, arousing her with hard and fast strokes.

She reached into the loose waistband of his pants, slipping them over his hips, filling her hands with the tensed curves of his ass. Her fingers played in the dimples at the sides there, loving the contrast between his lean perfection and her slightly fleshy backside.

He stood to remove this one last barrier, giving her another look at his distinctly male perfection.

"Okay?" He stared down at her. She couldn't believe he was

still unconvinced after their bout of sex on the floor. But he wasn't. And she almost resented him bringing the moments she was trying to forget back into theirs.

She tried to understand his need for reassurance. He simply wanted to make sure she was fine. Why should that upset her?

"No."

His eyes widened and his abs rippled. His hands curled into fists and he started to move away.

"I need you closer."

With a sighing groan he stepped back to her, but before he could kneel at her side, she reached a hand out and stopped him. She was at the perfect height, the perfect angle, to really study him.

She leaned toward him, running a single finger down his length from tip to base. She'd read books, watched movies, had sex as a teenager. She wasn't completely unfamiliar with the sexually aroused male. However, she was new to Chris. To the way he reacted to her touch, the way he jerked against her hand.

Her mouth watered, her lips plump and swollen. Everywhere he'd felt hard, rough…male. But here—she darted her tongue out, touching it to the tip of him and licking away the bead of moisture there—he was smooth, hot and strangely sweet.

She opened her mouth to take him inside, the desire to experience that part of him with her tongue and teeth difficult to ignore. Why should she?

The groan that echoed through his chest reverberated deep inside her own body. She enjoyed the way he filled her mouth and throat, felt her own sex weep at being left bereft of that same sensation.

He let her play for several minutes before pulling back on a ragged breath. "You need to stop."

Scooting back on the bed, she opened her arms and said, "Then come here."

He reached for her, drawing her up off the bed and plundering her mouth in a kiss that left her mind totally blank. He buried his hands deep in her hair, pulling her to him, pulling her tight. She relished the warmth that surged up at his touch; there was something entirely intimate and familiar about it.

His fingers slid inside her, testing. Once, just one experience with him, and the sensation was as familiar to her as her home. Her body pulsed, throbbed and tightened around him, searching for more.

She urged him toward the ache deep inside, spreading her legs wide. And as he slipped into her the barest inch, Karyn thought no matter what else happened, this moment was worth any price she'd pay, now or later.

Heat, throbbing pleasure and a blinding ache centered at her sex, shattering her entire focus. The sensation of him, hot and hard, filled everything.

She wrapped her legs around his waist. "More."

For once he listened, sliding completely inside with one long, controlled thrust that locked their hips tight. Her body stretched around him.

Reaching for him, she savaged his mouth with her own, putting every ounce of her liberation into the experience.

He moved inside her, slowly at first, but quicker, faster, harder as dug her heels into the backs of his thighs and urged him on. Everything vanished but the pleasure and friction of him deep inside her, making her shudder. A burning ache consumed her. The drive for fulfillment thrust her hips higher and higher.

"You're incredible, do you know that?"

Her muscles clamped around him. The spiraling edge of release grayed the boundaries of her sanity, sucking her into an alternate universe where only she and Chris existed. "I don't need words, Chris. I need you."

His pace quickened into a frenzy of passion. A ball of tension pulled at the small of her back, arching it farther than she'd ever thought it could go. Pleasure infused her senses.

His teeth scraped her nipple, and that simple action vaulted her into oblivion. But even as her own release burst through her, somewhere in the back of her mind she waited.

Her body clamped around him, the feel of him deep inside already reassuring and familiar. His guttural groan sounded in her ear. He thrust into her once, twice, three times before rearing back. Through half-closed lids she watched the power of his release, and knew she'd never experience a more perfect moment.

"How was that?"

Chris wasn't normally the type to need affirmation over his sexual performance. He'd done it enough times to recognize when a woman had been satisfied.

Karyn had found satisfaction, no doubt.

But there was more at stake for her than simple sexual gratification. Which was why he found himself asking the inane question.

"Amazing."

He couldn't help the burst of relief. "You're okay. No… worries?"

He walked a fine edge between assuring himself she was okay and bringing up memories neither of them wanted sharing their bed.

"I'm fine, Chris. Really. The only thing wrong right now is that you're interrupting my afterglow."

She said it with such a straight face he couldn't help but laugh.

"All right. I get it."

He pulled her into his arms, covered their naked bodies with the sheet and enjoyed the feel of her head against his shoulder. Predawn light teased at the window, but he didn't want to let it in. They had a few hours to enjoy the warmth of a shared bed before their day would begin.

His hands played with the ends of her hair. She sighed, the tiny tickle of her breath stirring across his chest. Her eyes drifted shut.

And his mind replayed every moment.

He hadn't meant to take things this far tonight. But she seemed fine.

He had a moment's guilt before he let her even breaths wash it away. Everything had worked out. Karyn had gotten what she'd wanted. He'd enjoyed amazing sex for the first time in months, longer if he admitted the women he'd slept with lately hadn't truly held his interest.

Unfortunately, Karyn held more than his interest. Because even as she dropped into a deep sleep beside him, Chris came to a startling realization. While his mind was still trying to figure things out, his body had taken over, dropped his defenses and left him open and vulnerable.

Karyn was like no other woman he'd ever met—brave, confident, beautiful and stronger than she realized. In fact, her quiet strength reminded him more and more of the mother he'd watched waste away and die with nothing but a smile to combat the fear.

Karyn was everything that had been missing from his life, everything his mother would have wanted for him. And he had no idea how to deal with her, or the unfamiliar emotions she stirred inside.

"WAKE UP, SLEEPYHEAD."

Karyn groaned, pulling the covers over her head against the too-cheerful sound.

The litany of incoherent mutters that grumbled through her buried lips became a shriek as the covers flew away and cold air doused her naked skin. Before the comforter and blanket could hit the floor, she was bounding out of the bed.

"What the he—"

Chris stopped the words in her throat with a breath-stealing kiss. By the time he let her up for air she was nowhere close to cold.

"That was mean." Karyn buried her face in the center of his chest and took a deep breath. Dirty tricks aside, there was something entirely pleasant about waking up with this man to warm her.

"I thought you were a morning person."

Glancing over his shoulder, she took in the nice, big numbers on the bedside clock. "That requires more than three hours of sleep, Dr. Desire."

"Sorry. Couldn't let you sleep the day away."

"I can think of a couple of nicer—" her lips curved into a mischievous smile against his skin "—ways you could have woken me up."

"Yes, but if I'd done that, we'd never have made it out of that bed."

Karyn rolled her head up, peeking at him through her half-shielded eyes. "What's wrong with that?"

Standing there, with her arms tucked between their bodies, his wrapped around her waist…it was amazing how quickly things could change. A month ago she'd never thought to experience this moment, the morning after, with anyone. And now it felt so right.

"Nothing. But it's our last day here and I didn't want you to miss all the fun."

Karyn's body tightened beneath his hold. It was Sunday. This afternoon they would head home. She had work. He had a show. She tried not to let the disappointment spoil the happy moment.

"All the more reason to stay in bed."

With a wicked grin, she reached for him, realizing that once again he was fully clothed while she had not a stitch on.

Ever evasive, he moved out of her grasp. "I have a surprise." Clasping her wrists and holding them uselessly over her head, he pulled her back against him. "I planned this before we came and I'd really hate for you to miss it."

"A surprise?" Her eyes widened in little-girl delight. She always had loved surprises. She just hadn't experienced any good ones in the past several years.

His smile said everything she needed to know. Her happiness pleased him—and that touched her.

"Wear jeans and sturdy shoes."

"Mmm, sounds romantic."

Chris nibbled at her lips. "It will be." He wanted to take the kiss further; she could feel his muscles tensing with arousal and recognized the sensation stirring in her own body, as well. It would be easy to do it—to open her mouth, her body, her soul to him.

But she couldn't do that. Not if she wanted to survive the moment they said goodbye.

Besides, she'd miss the surprise.

"Are you going to let me go so I can get dressed or are you gonna keep me wrist-shackled to you for the rest of the day?"

Chris's eyes turned hot as he took a measured step backward. His gaze raked across her body, every naked inch. She tingled, a slow, rolling burn that started in the pit of her stomach and fanned out.

"While the idea is appealing, and the view spectacular, I think it might be difficult to ride that way."

"Ride? Didn't we do that yesterday? I'd much rather stay in bed and ride you."

His eyes darkened and smoldered at her words. She loved the way they turned the colors of a roiling, smoke-filled sky when he was aroused. And she loved the knowledge that she could cause that change.

"Hot-air balloon. We're going to have a picnic."

13

KARYN'S BREATH CAUGHT at the sight below them. The world looked small and insignificant, so different from way up here. She could see for forever. It was everything she'd imagined, beautiful, calm and exhilarating.

But sharing those moments with Chris made them so much more.

He wrapped his arms around her as they looked at the slow-moving scenery beneath them. Her heart would jump at the startling sound of the burner or the terrifying height as he urged her to lean over the edge of the basket and look down. Each time, almost as if he could feel the reaction inside her, Chris had done something to distract her—brushed a hand against her breast, kissed the nape of her neck, whispered wicked innuendos in her ear.

It hadn't taken her long to realize part of the reason he held her so tight was to hide his gigantic hard-on from the pilot—a man who probably already thought they were lecherous newlyweds after all the groping and kissing.

By the time they landed, she was on the verge of exploding. The chase crew had driven Chris's SUV along with their truck. After helping them deflate and load the balloon, they experienced a ballooning tradition—having champagne dumped over their heads. Still laughing, they waved the pilot and crew away.

"I'm sticky." Karyn turned to Chris, accusation in her voice. "Did you know about that?"

"Maybe." Going to the back of the truck, he pulled out two towels, a blanket and a humongous picnic basket.

When he held out one towel, she snatched it from his hand and frowned, although she couldn't hold the expression for long. The day was simply too perfect. This morning she'd had sex, and now she'd lived out a childhood dream.

Couldn't get much better than this.

Karyn rubbed futilely at her arms, then her head to try to blot the dripping champagne from the ends of her hair. "This isn't going to help much. I might be dry, but I'm still sticky."

A startled sigh escaped out as Chris's tongue snaked a line across her exposed neck. "I can help with that."

He grabbed her around the waist, backing her tight against his erection.

"We're out in the open here, Chris. Anyone can see us." For heaven's sake, the ballooning people had just left. What if they'd forgotten something? They could come back at any minute.

Chuckling, he picked her up, rolling her around like a rag doll until he held her against his front, one arm at her back, one beneath her knees.

"There's no one here but us. Trust me—I grew up about thirty minutes away. I used to spend my summers up here, running wild through the fields, fishing in the creeks, building forts in the trees."

"Sounds like a great childhood."

"There were moments."

His voice held no conviction. In fact, she recognized the underlying tinges of anger and pain. She'd heard them in her own voice just last night when she'd talked about her rape. It had never occurred to her that perhaps Chris hadn't had the ideal life, either.

He had everything, money, fame, fans; he seemed to be comfortable and happy…

She opened her mouth to ask, wanting to know what had caused him pain, but before she could, he silenced her with his lips.

It didn't take long for his mouth to take her under, for his kiss to block out the world, for the ever-present heat to explode into a fire that took her breath away with its intensity.

Minutes later a loud rumble erupted between their bodies, pulling them out of that all-consuming daze. With a sheepish look down, she glared at her tattletale stomach.

"Food first." Chris nipped at her neck. "Then sex."

They ate quickly. She barely tasted the food he'd brought, only interested in sating one hunger in order to fulfill another.

Shoving leftovers out of the way, she crawled across the blanket straight for Chris.

Her body hummed, a pleasant sensation that had been her constant companion all morning. Reaching for her, Chris tucked her against his side and rolled them both to the ground.

The grass had started to brown and fade, losing its summer lushness to the unrelenting heat. They'd spread out beneath the shade of a large oak tree, hoping the branches would give them a little relief.

At the moment, the heat she felt had nothing to do with the August sun. And the relief she wanted had little to do with shade. What she did need was to be rid of the hot, clinging denim.

As if reading her mind, Chris unsnapped her jeans and pulled them from her body. The stiff material and silk panties beneath peeled off in a single sticky mess, leaving her with nothing to do but sigh at the liberation.

Her shirt and bra came next, followed quickly by his clothes. An unusual breeze kicked up, taking some of the oppressive heat with it.

Not that Karyn had felt it, anyway. The only thing she was aware of was the comfortable, heavy weight of Chris above her body. The long length of his erection nudging gently at the opening of her sex. The perfect way he filled her.

A storm kicked up, inside and out. In the distance, thunder rumbled, but she ignored it. They'd be leaving soon. This might be their last time together, nothing would take it away.

What if Chris was the only man who could make her feel this way? It was only an afternoon shower, and a little rain never hurt anyone.

He pushed them both to the edge, holding back to prolong the erotic pleasure. Karyn's muscles bunched, she could feel them tighten in anticipation of letting go. She held on, willing back the explosion, wanting every last second of bliss.

A single drop of water plopped onto her leg. Her eyes popped open at the surprising sensation. She looked up into a swirling sky, bright blue warring with dark gray, and couldn't hold back anymore. It reminded her so much of Chris's eyes right as orgasm took over.

She stared up into him as pleasure, pain, fear and love rolled around inside her. Her body convulsed with the power of her release even as Chris bucked above her in his.

Her heart pounded hard and fast, the booming thunder nothing compared to the sound in her ears. This time there was no sensation of peace, no feeling of finally breaking through that barrier. This time there really was fear…just not from the past.

She didn't want to let him go. No matter what she'd promised him, a few more hours, days, even weeks, weren't nearly enough. Would never be enough.

In that one moment of weakness, words slipped out that she hadn't meant to say. "I don't want to go home."

A BOLT OF LIGHTNING ripped open the sky, and the rain poured. They were soaked in minutes, puddles of water collecting in the seats and floorboards of his SUV when they finally made it there.

Even as the day darkened and the rain came down, the air around them thickened with humidity—and tension. Karyn's words hung between them.

It was difficult to breathe against the band tightening his chest. He was so far out on a limb here it wasn't even funny.

He didn't want to return to reality, either.

He'd done what she asked, cured her sexual inhibitions, shown her there was absolutely nothing wrong with her sex drive. And now the thought of her sharing those moments with another man, of him touching her skin, kissing her mouth, sliding home deep inside her body, made him want to snarl.

He'd never cared in the past, had never been possessive of any woman who'd shared his bed. They were free to do as they pleased, and so was he.

Karyn was different. She was his, damn it. And that scared him to death.

The urge to brand her, to mark her, surged up with a primitive force he couldn't ignore.

Turning, his sopping jeans squeaking a protest against wet leather, he grasped her by the waist, lifted her bodily from the seat and pulled her tight into his lap. Despite having just made love, his need for her hadn't slackened. In fact, it raged higher and hotter than he'd ever thought possible.

His fingers bit into her arms. Her eyes went round with shock before melting into deep, dark pools of chocolate lust. His cock jerked as her body melted, too, flowing against him in wet, warm surrender. Her immediate response drew a growl from deep inside.

"Then stay. I want you to stay."

Grasping the back of her neck through wet, heavy hair, he

pulled her head back, exposing her, making her vulnerable. His teeth grazed sharply down her throat. She sighed and closed her eyes in abandon.

"Okay."

It was possibly the single most erotic thing he'd ever seen, complete and total surrender, red curls rioting down her back, T-shirt soaked through with rain, dark pink nipples drawn tight and hard with chill and desire.

She smelled of wet grass and tasted of heaven, a sweet, fresh sip of renewing growth.

And he wanted more.

"Damn these car makers. Who needs ten cup holders?" She shifted her body, drawing her knees up tight against his, bringing her denim-covered sex in full contact with his straining erection. "That's better."

No. It wasn't. It wasn't enough. Would never be enough.

Ripping the soggy shirt from her body, he threw it into the floorboard beside them.

Wrapping his arms around her, he brought them flush together once again and pulled in a deep breath for the sheer joy of the sensation. The feel of his chest rising and falling against hers sent a thrill of sensation rushing down.

Her skin was rain cooled and soft. The tiny, tight points of her nipples thrust against his chest, making it ache, making him ache. She wrapped her arms around his neck and held on.

"At least the rain washed off the champagne. That stuff was sticky."

"Maybe, but I hadn't finished licking it off. I got distracted."

She laughed, the sound twanging his chest before reverberating lower.

"Then lick the rain."

And he did, inch by excruciating inch. By the time he finally reached her nipples the water on her body had evaporated into steam. With a flick of his tongue, he took several lapping licks before pulling one tight peak into his mouth.

She gasped at the tug of his teeth.

She writhed against him, riding the ridge of his erection and driving them both insane.

The jeans, they had to go. Pushing her up on her knees, Chris fought the wet denim until they finally bunched down her thighs. It probably would have made things easier if he'd taken the time to pull them off completely, but the throbbing at the apex of his thighs wouldn't wait.

She didn't seem to mind. In fact, she was busy herself, tearing at his own zipper. She had him freed in seconds flat, and before he could utter a word, dropped back down, taking him fully inside.

The jolt of her seared through him. He was buried straight up to her womb.

With a drowning groan, Chris wrapped his arms beneath her rear, changing her angle, holding her tighter.

So close. He was so close. But he didn't think he could hold back much longer, not when she felt so perfect.

He rained kisses over her chest, the sides of each breast, the valley between. Licking, biting, urging them both on.

He couldn't move, stuck between her and the unforgiving seat at his back. He wanted to, wanted to drive hard and high against her, to lose himself inside her and simply let it all go.

Grabbing the damp leather behind his head, Karyn levered herself up and off. His muscles convulsed at the agonizing loss of her wet heat.

He knew what she was doing, prolonging the pleasure, but at the moment he didn't care. What he wanted was to feel every squeeze of her muscles milking him dry as she flew apart around him.

Grasping her hips, he leaned her into the steering wheel and slid back home.

Her body immediately bunched around him, a prelude to the explosion to come. And even as the smallest ripples broke through her body, a sound, the complaining, intrusive sound of the car horn, echoed through his brain.

He ignored it as his own body jolted with release. He thrust inside her one last time, sliding from the crest of the wave, enjoying her tiny sigh of satisfaction as she fell limply back into his lap.

He gathered her close, tucking her head beneath his chin.

She was his.

KARYN WOKE SLOWLY, the realization that she wasn't alone seeping in with the early-morning light. She stretched, her arms brushing against warm male flesh as she went.

A bubble of contentment settled somewhere in the center of her chest and a half-formed smile tugged at her lips. Warm and cozy, she rolled against Chris, wanting nothing more than to stay right where she was all day.

"Good morning."

"Hmm." Too comfortable even to make the effort for one word, the sound died in the back of her throat.

He shifted beside her, his arm snaking around her waist, pulling her in tighter against his body.

They took their time drifting awake and when Karyn opened her eyes she found herself gazing directly into his.

There was a light, an intensity there that she hadn't seen before. And wouldn't see again. Today was it. In a few hours they'd drive home, he'd drop her at her apartment and she'd never see him again.

He'd fulfilled his promise. She was sexually whole. It wasn't his fault that when he left there would now be a new hole in her heart.

She swallowed hard and tried on a bright smile. It felt fake.

She was afraid he'd seen through her attempt when he clamped his arms around her tight, and tucked them both back beneath the covers.

But he didn't say anything. Instead, they lay together, wrapped in silence and each other. Pleasure blended with misery as the feel of his hand stroking easily up and down her back made her heart ache and her body hum.

"Stay with me tonight."

His words surprised her, and sent a thrill of hope down her spine before she crushed it. Chris seemed almost as surprised by the words as she was.

"Why?"

"We can spend the day in town, head back to my place. I have a show tonight, but…you'll be there when I get back. We can pick up your car or I can take you to work in the morning. One more night to make sure my job is complete."

His blue eyes smiled down at hers, the gray and green flecks shimmering in the morning light.

She'd been right. He hadn't meant the offer the way she'd hoped. But she couldn't seem to stop herself from asking, "Just tonight?" And despised herself for the edge of need she heard in those two words.

"I've really enjoyed our weekend. I'm not ready for it to end."

Neither was she, but wouldn't spending the night with him just put off the moment when she'd watch him walk away? Was she being greedy? Asking for trouble? Tempting fate?

As if sensing her internal debate, Chris leaned across the space between them and pushed her with a deep kiss. It was an invasion of her mind and will because as he let her go she heard herself say, "Okay."

He rewarded her with another kiss. As his tongue plundered her mouth, her mind spewed rationalizations.

It would be fine. What was the worst that could happen?

14

THEY DROVE BACK late that afternoon, stopping for a quick bite at a roadside place along the way. Karyn knew their weekend was coming to an end, but she didn't expect the veneer of peacefulness she had wrapped around herself—thin though it might have been—to break almost the minute they walked through Chris's front door.

The abbreviated tour of his place, punctuated by stolen kisses and a brief bout of groping in the kitchen, came to an abrupt end in the back hallway when Karyn's heel crunched on shards of broken glass.

"Call 911 then get next door." Chris shoved his cell into her hand as he thrust her unceremoniously out the door. She couldn't decide whether to be pissed or scared because he hadn't joined her.

She'd just finished giving the operator what little information she knew when he came through his doorway. The tightness at the back of her throat that she'd been fighting to talk through eased.

"Damn it!"

Without even thinking about the gesture, she closed the gap between them and wrapped her arms tightly around him.

"I'm so sorry, Chris. Was anything taken?"

Every muscle in his body was tense.

"Nothing of value. Just my toothbrush and some dirty clothes."

"Toothbrush? Clothes?" Karyn didn't understand.

"It was a fan. My number-one fan according to the lipstick message on my bathroom mirror." Raking a hand through his hair, he growled deep in the back of his throat.

"They're sending the police. They should be here shortly."

"No hurry. Whoever it was is long gone."

In a twisted version of déjà vu, Karyn sat next to Chris as two policemen questioned him. When she'd reported the rape, she hadn't liked being interviewed, being repeatedly asked to recall the details they'd needed. Watching Chris wasn't any picnic, either.

She read frustration in his eyes, on his face and in the way he clenched and unclenched his hands into fists.

Finally they left, leaving little comfort or hope behind. No prints. No evidence. Nothing much to go on. The cops did say they'd check with the neighbors, but Karyn didn't get the impression they expected to find anything.

It made her blood run cold. She'd never realized how exposed Chris was, how being Dr. Desire could touch every aspect of his life. He couldn't escape even here at home.

"You ready to go?"

She looked up into his eyes, a cloudy, unhappy blue. "Go?"

"I'll drop you home on my way to the station."

She'd heard him arguing with Michael earlier about whether the show should continue tonight as planned. Chris had obviously won.

"Why?"

"Because it's not safe."

"Chris, I'm fine. It's fine. Go do the show. I'll wait for you here."

"No. You—"

"You heard the police, whoever it was isn't violent. They just wanted a souvenir. I'll be okay. Besides, they'll be in the neighborhood if I really need them."

For the last two hours she'd watched Chris deal with the mess this person had left him. He spent his life working so hard to help others, to provide a place where they could ask questions and get answers in a safe environment. No, he wasn't bringing about world peace or putting an end to war. But he did try to improve people's lives. And in return his home had been vandalized.

In her heart Karyn knew it wasn't nearly the same, but part of her identified with the sense of violation he must be experiencing. She would not let this person, this inconsiderate and selfish idiot, take one more thing from him. Especially not their last night together.

He must have seen the determination in her eyes because after a few more attempted arguments, all of which she immediately shot down, he gave in, very reluctantly.

Checking—and rechecking—every lock on every door and window, Chris finally left. She stared down at the list of neighbor's phone numbers and felt a smile playing at her lips. If he was this concerned about her…what would he be like with a woman he truly loved?

Cutting the thought out because it hurt too much, she walked around the place, really seeing it for the first time since they'd come through the door. She recognized the unmistakable touches of a man's hand in the pool table located in the dining room, the deer head over the living room fireplace, the dark colors and the abundance of leather and electronics. But underneath that there was a sense of home.

And her heart ached because she knew some of that feeling of security would now be gone.

Unable not to look, she headed for the bathroom off the master suite. Smears of red with flecks of white dotted the silvery surface of the mirror, as if someone had scraped off the message with toilet paper, managing to spread the mess around more rather than wipe it away. But the words were gone, which was probably all Chris had cared about at that moment. She'd find some window cleaner and remove the remaining traces before he got home.

Looking around at the rest of the space, Karyn couldn't suppress a feeling of surprise. She'd expected something austere, almost cold, maybe chrome and glass, angles and sharp edges. Instead, a large, hand-tiled bathtub was centered on one wall beneath a large picture window. The dark colors had bled into here, as well, but beautiful marbled tiles of beige, burgundy and sandy-brown muted their effect. The space was pretty, relaxing.

God, that bathtub looked like heaven—that she could see herself sitting in it, waiting for Chris to return home from a show was not a good thing.

Stepping from the room, she picked up her purse, fished out her cell phone, turned it on and dialed Anne. She needed something else to think about.

"Where the hell are you?"

Her friend's greeting startled her. "I'm at Chris's place, why?"

"Because everyone and their brother seemed to be looking for you today and they all decided I was your keeper."

Karyn groaned. "I hope you didn't tell anyone where I was."

"You think I'm an idiot? One of the people asking for you was your boss."

"But I called him, told him I was taking a vacation day."

"Yeah, but he needed to ask you a question and thought I might know where you were."

"Oh, well, he'll get over it."

"Yeah, he will, but your mother might not."

"My mother? What does she have to do with this?" Even as she asked the question she knew she really didn't want to know the answer.

"Apparently she was looking for you, too. I had to do some pretty fancy footwork in order to convince her you weren't tied to the bed by some pervert."

Karyn closed her eyes and sagged against the wall. That's just what she needed, her mother in protective overdrive. "What did you tell her? Every single word."

Her friend's exasperated tone registered, but Karyn had more important things to worry about—like whether her mother was going to show up on her doorstep in the middle of the night.

"I told her that you'd gone out of town to relax and unwind."

On the surface that sounded pretty inconsequential—if she hadn't told her mother she was so busy at work she probably couldn't even get time off for Labor Day weekend. Oh, well, there wasn't much she could do about it now.

"Thanks for covering for me, Anne." Karyn tried to keep the slight edge out of her voice. It really wasn't her friend's fault that she'd unwittingly placed a land mine at her feet.

She supposed a trip home over Labor Day wouldn't be so bad.

"Will you be in tomorrow?"

She probably should go to work, but something told her she was going to need a day to rest and recuperate from the weekend. She hadn't gotten much sleep and she seriously doubted she'd be catching up tonight.

"Probably not."

"You want to tell me how things went?"

"Maybe, but not tonight." She wanted to keep the details to herself right now. She wasn't ready to share.

"Well, do me a favor and leave your cell on. I'm tired of being your secretary."

Karyn laughed, promised she would and hung up. Heading back downstairs, she went to find a radio so she could listen to Chris's show. If he couldn't be there with her in person, at least she could hear his voice.

A large, built-in bookcase occupied the entire length of the den. Stacks of books, racks of movies and CDs, several gleaming statues and knickknacks all shared the space along with the most high-tech audio system she'd ever seen. She was surprised, although why she wasn't sure. He did make his living on the radio.

She was almost afraid to touch it, but she played with switches, dials and buttons until his station's call numbers popped onto the digital display and rock music entered the room. Listening for a moment, letting the throbbing sounds soak into her skin, she began trailing her hands across the other things on the shelf.

She was about to turn away and explore more of his home when something stopped her. A book out of line with the others. Her eyes scanned down the spine, reading the words twice before she processed them: *Sexual Abuse, Understanding and Recovery.*

She stared at the dark blue letters on the silver spine. Pulling it gently from the shelf, she dropped onto the large leather sectional with a plop that echoed through the room. Opening the book, her fingers ran down the index page, registering chapter headings without really reading them.

She flipped through page after page, her fingers shaking, until she reached the end and several pieces of folded paper fell into her lap.

Karyn stared at them for several minutes before picking them up. Did she really want to know what they said?

Black letters, messy, scrunched, covered the page. She couldn't read some of the notes, the handwriting was that bad, but there was no mistaking the list toward the bottom of the page.

Step 1—Non sexual touches

Step 2—Personal sexual touches

Step 3—Mutual sexual touches with no intercourse

Step 4—Intercourse

Her heart squeezed. Steps. He'd devised steps for her. Drawn up a plan. Like a pet project. A flush of heat, a very unpleasant one, flew up her skin.

She flipped to the next page, skimming down, picking out a word here and there: "masturbate," "naked," "away."

Familiar theme music filled the room, snapping her attention from the paper and over to the stereo. Chris's voice followed swiftly behind. "I hope everyone had a wonderful weekend, I certainly did."

She'd been his weekend project. Most guys built bookshelves or changed the oil in their car. Apparently Dr. Desire had decided sex with the rape victim would offer a new, exciting challenge.

"We're in for an interesting night. We have several callers on the line with questions and stories to share. Stick around—it's going to be a wild ride."

Wild ride. She turned her focus back to the paper in her hand and continued reading—or trying to.

"Sharon from Georgia is on the line. Let's find that spark in your love life."

"Dr. Desire, how can I make a man commit? I've been dating the same guy for three years now, the sex is fantastic, we practically live together, but he will not propose."

"Sharon, I can honestly say this is the question women stop me on the street to ask most. There's a simple answer, but unfortunately no one likes to hear it. Men who want to commit do, the ones who don't won't. There isn't anything you can do or say. What you need out of the relationship is something he can't or won't give you. Get out."

"What if I don't want to?"

"Then stop complaining, stop hoping and enjoy what you have. The question is are you happy with what's in front of you? If the answer's no, then leave."

Karyn's eyes zeroed in on that list.

For the first time in longer than she could remember, tears prickled the backs of her eyes. She blinked them away, tipped back her head and tried to hold them inside. The last time she'd cried, standing in a deserted courtroom, feeling foolish and betrayed, she'd promised herself she wouldn't ever cry again. Crying accomplished nothing.

And here she was, about to cry over her own stupidity. She'd known what would happen. She'd known her time with him would only last a few days. But she'd been brainless and, somewhere along the way, had left her heart open and vulnerable.

But she couldn't be mad at Chris. She was the one who'd broken the rules. Not to mention her promise. It wasn't his fault; he'd done precisely what she'd asked of him.

She'd been the one to fall in love.

While he was following some sexual instruction manual she'd let herself become emotionally invested. She'd lied, not only to him, but herself. And she'd bought her own story—hook, line and sinker.

She did want a normal life, husband, family, kids. But not with anyone. With him.

Karyn looked around his den, complete with brown leather, silver electronics, dead deer and navy blue walls. The place was a bachelor pad and always would be.

She couldn't stay. Her heart crumpled inside her chest. She saw the space around her, Chris stamped on every square inch. She could have fit in here, could see herself cooking him dinner in the kitchen, sleeping in his bed, listening to his voice through the speakers of that radio.

But that would never happen. Because he would never see her that way, as anything more than a weekend challenge. And the longer she stayed, the more leaving would hurt.

Karyn had always thought the night she'd been raped would be the worst of her life.

The tearing pain in her chest as she gathered her bags, wrote a note and locked the door behind her before calling Anne, couldn't compare to the humiliation, guilt and self-recrimination she'd felt five years ago.

This pain was so much worse.

DARRELL SAT IN A DARK CORNER of the station parking lot. He tried to ignore the edge of desperation that seemed to swim up every time he sat too long. He'd just spent his last dollar buying a cup of coffee at the place down the street. Bad coffee—and now he didn't have a single penny to his name.

Popping open his glove compartment, he stared at the dull black finish on the pistol he'd stashed there. It was a possession, one of many he'd thrown into a suitcase when he'd finally gotten access to his stuff. At the time he hadn't thought much about it.

But over the past few days a realization had niggled at the back of his brain.

He was Chris's sole living relative. If, and it was a big if, the boy didn't have a will—if some unfortunate accident happened—he'd inherit everything from Dr. Desire. He'd never have to fear being in this situation again.

Was he ready to take the risk—that he'd get caught, or that Chris would leave every possession to some bleeding heart cause like the local orphanage?

Slamming the glove compartment door home, he decided no. Not when he had a hunch he could play instead.

Hours of sitting in this damn car, waiting for any sign of his son and that woman, had left him plenty of time to think. He'd lost their trail the night he jumped from the window, his heart sounding a sickening thud in his ears.

Somewhere in the dark of night he'd realized something: his son had been hiding the girl in that secluded resort town. Why else would they have separate cabins? Dr. Desire wouldn't let a woman sleep yards away without an ulterior motive.

If she was that rape victim…it was the only thing that made sense to him. But he had no proof.

However, Chris didn't need to know that.

CHRIS WALKED OUT of the station into a dark midnight. There were few stars and only a sliver of moon to cut through the night. The parking lot was practically deserted, occupied mostly by the cars of the skeleton crew for the station. Michael had stayed behind, saying he needed to finish up a couple things before he headed home for the night.

Walking alone out here didn't bother him though. In fact, it offered him a moment to stretch his back, clear his head and anticipate what waited for him at home.

Karyn.

Several times tonight he'd thought about her. He'd had the urge to discuss a particular caller with her or get her opinion on his advice. The vision of her naked in his bed waiting for him, ready to help him unwind, had popped into his brain at the most inopportune moments.

His mind was halfway home before he even reached his car. Which was why when his father stepped out of the shadows he nearly jumped out of his skin.

"Good show tonight, Dr. Desire."

Darrell smiled, but the expression reminded Chris more of a hungry shark than a proud father. He was really sick of the man popping in and out of his life. It might actually be worth a few thousand dollars to get him to crawl back under whatever rock he'd come from.

And then the memory of his mother, thin and pale against white hospital sheets resurfaced and killed that thought stone dead.

"You're really enjoying your success, aren't you?" Darrell stepped around the nose of Chris's Porsche to plant his butt on the hood and cross his arms over his chest. If anyone else had done that, Chris probably would have laid them out flat. But somehow he thought that was what his father wanted. Which was why he stood there with a raised eyebrow and a bored look on his face.

"It'd be a shame to lose all this, wouldn't it? The fancy car, nice house, fans, friends, fame. What about that little redhead? Would she be so interested in you without your money? That quick getaway? Fancy cabin?"

His father's eyes gleamed and Chris's stomach rolled. But he wouldn't give the man the satisfaction of knowing he'd hit his mark. How did he know about the cabin?

He must have followed them. That was the only explanation. But if he knew about their trip to Morganville, what else did he know?

"I'm really not sure what you're talking about."

Darrell stood up. "Oh, I think you do. That pretty little redhead… Was her name Katy or Karyn? I can't remember which."

Chris felt a spurt of panic before he locked it back down.

"What do you want?" His hands shook with rage and fear as he slipped them into his back pockets.

Not fear of the man before him, but of what he could strip away. With one flippant move his father could take everything that mattered.

Karyn had been through so much already in her life. She'd endured the humiliation of having her worst nightmare relived and dissected on a regular basis by people who didn't care. He'd do anything in his power to prevent that from happening to her again.

After all those lonely years, he'd finally found what he'd lost when his mother died. He'd be damned if he'd let the bastard take Karyn away, too. And that's precisely what could happen if the media got hold of her story, of her link to him. She'd be embarrassed and angry and might think he'd sold her out for publicity and his show.

"What I wanted before—money. Only, now the price has gone up."

Chris seethed. His jaw clamped down so tight, the back of his head ached with the pressure. "How much?"

"Fifty thousand."

Chris couldn't believe he was even considering this. But in his heart he knew there wasn't a choice. Whatever his father wanted he'd give him.

It would kill Karyn to see herself, naked and vulnerable, splashed all over the newspapers and televisions. She'd run from one life, embarrassed and fed up with the intrusion. He'd promised her safety and protection. Fifty thousand dollars was a small price to pay in order to keep that promise.

"After tonight, I never want to see you again." Chris reached for the other man, hauling him physically up off the car. Their faces were centimeters apart. Chris dragged air into his lungs and fought back the desire to bury a fist into his father's face.

"Whatever you say."

"I'll write you a check."

"I want cash."

"I don't keep that kind of cash lying around."

"What assurance do I have that it's good?"

Chris gave a bitter laugh. "That I'm a better man than you."

Darrell shook his head.

"Take it or leave it."

The man stared at him, hard. The muscles in his arms bunched as if he were about to jerk away and leave. A bowling ball dropped into Chris's stomach as he feared he was about to be called on his bluff.

Instead, his father said, "Fine. Start writing."

He worked hard at not letting out a sigh of relief. Reaching for his wallet, he flipped open his checkbook and began to write. The rip of the check leaving the book echoed loudly through the deserted lot. He held the flimsy paper out, but instead of letting it go when Darrell grabbed the other end, his hand flashed out and squeezed the man around the throat.

"If you so much as think about breathing a word of what you know after you have my money, I'll kill you with my bare hands and drop your sorry ass off a cliff. No one cares about you. No one would ever miss you. Do you understand me?"

His father simply nodded, staring at him with the cold gray eyes so similar to his own.

Chris watched the man walk away, slip into his own red car and leave.

He stood still in the surrounding darkness. A moment ago his life had been great. Now his heart raced inside his chest and bile rose at the back of his throat. Had he done the right thing?

Yes. Yes, he had. He'd promised Karyn safety; he'd whispered those words to her during the most intimate, open moment of his life. He would keep that promise.

No matter what it cost him.

15

CHRIS WALKED into his house, his stomach still rocking and rolling from the encounter with his father. But it was over.

He'd taken his father's word. He hated to do it but didn't have much choice. Aside from killing the man where he stood—something Chris wasn't willing to do, much as he was tempted—he could never be certain.

"Karyn?" He called gently through the house. It was late, almost two in the morning, and if she had fallen asleep he didn't want to wake her. At least not yet.

He moved through his home, enjoying the golden glow of the lamp she'd left burning in the den. It was nice to walk inside and know someone—Karyn—was there waiting. It was a sensation he'd never realized he had been missing.

Walking down the long hall, he headed to his own bedroom. There were no lights burning here, but moonlight filtered into the hallway. He could imagine it falling across Karyn's sleep-warmed cheeks, the curve of her shoulder and the swell of her hip beneath his sheets.

Only she wasn't there. Not in his bed asleep, not in his bathroom soaking in a bubble bath, not in his kitchen, the den, even the laundry room.

She wasn't there.

He stared through the lamplight. The same light that just moments ago had been warm and inviting now seemed lonely and weak. She wasn't there. But she'd left a note, lying in the center of his coffee table, atop the book he'd turned to so many times over the past week.

He picked it up and stared at the curling letters of his name pressed into the pristine white envelope. They were neat, perfect and held a sense of strength behind the feminine hand. Damn it, they were exactly what he'd expected from Karyn.

His heart wanted to believe that she'd just decided to go home for tonight, had been too tired after their weekend to stay awake. But he knew.

That book told it all.

Pulling the single sheet of paper, he read the brief lines.

Thank you. You'll never know how much I appreciate all that you've done for me. I need to move on with my life. I can't do that with you.
Karyn

Chris stared at the last line and felt the bottom drop out of his world for the second time in his life.

"Can't do that with you." No, she couldn't. Not when he had to turn to a book for advice on helping her. Not when he couldn't even contain himself long enough to follow the steps that book had outlined.

He'd failed in everything she'd asked him to do.

And he'd failed in something even worse—keeping his heart protected. Keeping himself detached and uncaring. Karyn had wormed her way through his defenses. She'd made him care, about her, about what she'd gone through, about the woman she wanted to be, the woman he could already see.

Damn it! She couldn't be gone. He'd spent his entire life making sure no one mattered, that he didn't need anyone and that they didn't need him. He'd been so afraid of being disappointed…or of disappointing someone important. But Karyn had slipped through, with those damn golden-brown eyes and that serene smile.

And now that she'd gotten what she needed from him that was it? So long, farewell, don't let the door hit you in the ass?

The hell she would! She might think she didn't need him anymore, but she did.

He sure as hell needed her.

THE PHONE RANG, pulling Chris from a groggy sleep.

He'd spent half the night trying to find Karyn; she hadn't been at her apartment. She'd either refused to answer his calls or had turned off her cell. The only person in her life he knew was Anne, but he had no idea what her last name was or where she lived. He'd spent a couple hours driving around the area of her apartment, hoping to find something…her car, her friend, anything.

At about 5:00 a.m. he'd given up and come home. She'd eventually showed up—at home or at work. It really didn't matter to him as long as he could convince her she was wrong. She could forget the past. He was the only one who could help her do that.

"Hello." His heart raced with the hope that Karyn had changed her mind.

But that hope died away as Michael's voice drifted down the line.

"I'm sorry to wake you, buddy, but I think you need to know about this. I just got a tip that the *news* is running a story on you and Katy—er, Karyn—this morning."

"What?" That had the fog clearing from his brain in two seconds flat. "What are you talking about?"

"They have the whole story. Much more than I was even aware existed."

Chris heard the simmering anger in his producer's voice.

"I think you'd better get in here fast. Legal's in an uproar. Not to mention Heath."

Twenty billion things skated through Chris's mind. He was going to kill his father—because there was no doubt in his mind where the information had come from.

Karyn was going to have a conniption fit. He had to find her, explain to her, before this one story blew whatever chance remained with her. She'd think it had been him.

"I'm sure you guys can handle this. I have to talk to Karyn."

"She's a big girl. Right now you need to get in here and do damage control if you want to keep your job."

"At the moment, I don't give a shit, Michael. You save my job. I have more important things to worry about." Like how he was going to find her this morning when he couldn't find her last night.

"What time is it?" He blurted the question out as he ran his eyes over the room trying to find a clock. Didn't he own a damn clock?

"Eight forty-five. Why?"

She'd be at work. He'd start there.

And while he was at it, he'd stop payment on that check he'd written his lying, cheating, son-of-a-bitch father.

DARRELL PULLED UP outside the bank branch. Whistling, he stepped out of his car, gave the middle-aged woman walking his way a million dollar smile and headed inside. The sun was shining, the sky was blue, and the check in his pocket was going to turn his fortunes right around.

He really hadn't wanted a check from Chris. But he'd taken it. Not only did he believe the boy didn't keep that kind of cash lying around, he seriously doubted his son had the balls to screw him over. Not and save the sensibilities of that pretty little redhead.

The story he'd sold to the newspaper wouldn't come out

until tomorrow, the brunette barracuda of a reporter had promised him. He'd be long gone with the money by then.

The clerk's eyes registered surprise for the briefest moment
as she looked down at the check he was trying to cash.

"Sir, do you have an account with our bank?"

"No. But the check's written on an account here." He knew
they would be able to cash it. He'd actually tried a bank down
the street, but they wouldn't handle it for him unless he opened
an account.

"I'll need you to fill out some forms, sir, while we verify
the account balance and I check with my branch manager on
how we can pay this."

"Fine, fine."

Darrell filled in the blank spaces, using the old information
still listed on his driver's license. The IRS could go after
Virginia when he didn't report the funds.

"Sir, I'm sorry, but we won't be able to cash the check for
you." He looked up from the black-specked countertop to the
dark-skinned woman behind.

"Why not?"

"A stop payment has been placed on this check."

Stop payment? What the hell had happened?

His no-good son had double-crossed him, that was what.

"That can't be right. There must be some mix-up."

"I'm sorry, sir, there isn't. According to our records, Mr.
Faulkner called early this morning to place a hold on this check."

He didn't remember what he said or how he got out of the
bank. His empty hands curled into fists as he sat in his Jag, the
suffocating summer heat already seeping inside. They wouldn't
even give him back the check so he could try and open an
account down the street.

Darrell's gaze darted around aimlessly before settling on the
week-old newspaper thrown haphazardly into the passenger

seat beside him. He picked it up, staring at the image of his son and that little redhead. Karyn Mitchell. He remembered the address on the driver's license at the cabin. She'd be easy enough to find.

And Chris needed to pay.

"JUST A MINUTE."

Karyn pulled the warm, fuzzy bathrobe tighter around her body and jerked the knot to be sure. The pounding on her front door had been so loud she'd heard it all the way inside her bathroom, despite the closed door.

Something about the noise set her spine on edge. She looked through the peephole, but didn't recognize the older man with jet-black hair standing on her porch.

"Who is it?"

"Karyn? I'm Darrell, Chris's dad. I need to talk to you."

Chris's dad? She didn't even know he had one. He'd mentioned his mother, but never his father. She'd just assumed the man was either dead or not a part of his life. Just more proof that he had never seen her as someone important. She'd shared the intimate details of her worst experience; he hadn't even mentioned a father living here in the city.

She looked back through the peephole again. She did recognize a certain resemblance between the two men. The eyes were the same blue-gray mix, and the tilt of his head, the way he held himself with controlled confidence, that was so like Chris.

Shrugging her shoulders, she opened the door but didn't invite him inside.

"What's wrong?"

"Chris has been in an accident. The hospital called me, but they said he was asking for you. Get dressed. I'll take you."

The man moved so smoothly past her, she wasn't even sure how it happened. One minute her arm had been across the open doorway, the next it was at her side and he was standing in the middle of her entranceway.

Chris had been in an accident and was asking for her? Why? She knew he'd called her cell phone last night. She'd turned it on briefly this morning and seen his missed call.

At the time she'd wondered what he could possibly want. Not that it mattered at the moment, not if he was hurt.

"Give me a minute." She ran into the bedroom and began throwing on the first things she found in the closet.

"What happened? Why was he out? He usually sleeps later than this after a show."

"I'm not real sure. The hospital didn't give me many details."

That was bad, right? If he was seriously injured they wouldn't tell his father that over the phone.

She raced out of the bedroom, hopping on one foot as she tried to tie her shoe. "I'm ready. Let's go."

Looking up, midhop, she froze. Darrell, pointing the black barrel of a handgun at her, leaned against her front door. The gun looked humongous, although it probably wasn't any bigger than normal. She had just never seen one…pointed at her chest.

"What are you doing? We need to get to the hospital."

"Chris is fine. For now. In fact, I'd really appreciate it if you called him. Get his sorry ass over here."

"Wait. What? I don't understand."

"What's there to understand? That sorry sack of shit you're screwing cheated me out of some money he owes me. I'd like to get it back. So pick up that phone—" he motioned with his empty hand toward the kitchen counter "—and call him before something irrevocable happens."

Karyn slowly put her foot down onto the floor, careful not to step on the still-dangling laces she hadn't finished tying. "What does this have to do with me?"

"Everything. Are you going to call him over here or are you going to spend months in the hospital recovering from reconstructive knee surgery?"

Part of her brain wanted to believe this man, Chris's father, wasn't capable of something like that. But she'd been through enough in her life to know that people were often capable of more sinister things than she'd expect.

"Okay." She held up her hands to signal she was cooperating and walked across to her phone. "What am I supposed to say to him?"

"I don't care, sweetheart. Why don't you tell him to come fuck your brains out? I'm sure he'll be over here in a flash."

Karyn winced. "We're not sleeping together."

"Bullshit. Tell that lie to someone who believes it."

"We're not sleeping together anymore."

"Then I guess you better come up with some other reason to get him over here. Fast."

Her fingers shook as she dialed Chris's home number. She hated the sign of weakness, but knew her body was only reacting to the adrenaline spilling into her blood. When his answering machine picked up, she dialed his cell.

He answered on the first ring.

"Karyn? Where are you? We need to talk."

A tight band squeezed her chest, constricting her heart, and made her lungs difficult to inflate. She wanted so much to tell a lie, to send him somewhere his father couldn't touch him. But that cold black hole stared at her from across the room.

She looked up into the other man's eyes, so like his son's, but saw something there she'd never seen in Chris. Hate and a crystal-clear frenzy of panic.

If she didn't do what he wanted, she had no doubt he'd pull the trigger and she'd end up injured…or dead.

"I'm at home, Chris." Karyn's throat tightened as she tried

to keep the tremor in her hands and legs from transferring to her voice. "Your father's here. He wants to talk to you."

"My father? Karyn, are you okay?"

She stared across at the other man, licked her suddenly dry lips and said, "No. He wants to talk in person."

"Karyn, I'm calling the police. Sit tight. I'll be there in a few minutes. Everything will be fine."

THE FIFTEEN MINUTES it took him to get from Karyn's office to her apartment felt like an eternity. He'd gone there looking for her, but had just found Anne when she'd called.

Cop cars bracketed the ends of her street and lined the spaces in front of her apartment. He'd expected chaos, noise, lights, sirens. Instead silence enveloped the entire street. There was a flurry of activity at one of the barricades. With a screeching halt that drew several stares, he pulled up next to it and jumped out.

He was halfway around a patrol car before someone reached out and grabbed his arm to stop him.

"I'm sorry, sir. You can't go in there. We have a hostage situation."

"Hostage?" Somewhere in the back of his mind he'd hoped it hadn't been true, for both Karyn's and his father's sakes. "That's my girlfriend's house. What happened?"

"Someone fired a gun through the front window as an officer approached."

Chris's heart collided with the bottom of his feet. "No." He tried to push past the man who stopped him with a single hand.

He looked up into the burly cop's face and registered the other man's regret as he said, "I'm sorry, sir. I can't let you do that. We have a team circling the perimeter to assess the situation."

"Assess? I'll tell you the situation. My father is holding my girlfriend in there. Now let me go so I can get inside."

Instead of doing as he'd asked, the officer caught the attention of a couple of colleagues and nodded them over. "He's the boyfriend and son. Take him over there and keep him company."

Despite being pissed and scared shitless, even Chris recognized the order beneath his words, *and don't let him out of your sight.*

Time seemed to come to a blaring halt. Every minute passed like an hour and every hour felt like a day off his life. The sun came up, crested and started down. The officers brought him a sandwich and sodas. He didn't taste any of it.

Farther down the street, he watched as a congregation of news trucks, with large antennae and raised satellites, set up camp nearby. He listened with half an ear to one noon news update. Apparently, the entire state was glued to the hostage situation involving Dr. Desire's latest fling—who just happened to be the rape victim who'd called into the show several weeks ago—and his estranged father.

The story his father had leaked, probably before he'd written the son of a bitch that check, was now being reported by each and every station. Some of them got the details wrong, having gleaned their information from nothing more than the early-morning paper.

Some of them got it right. There was speculation about love triangles, jealousy, implied misconduct. He listened as his life and childhood, what details they knew, were dissected, Karyn's experience scrutinized.

At about two o'clock in the afternoon, Chris looked up from the cup of soda he'd been staring into for what felt like hours and realized the scene around him was an honest to God circus.

He could see the edge of Karyn's porch down the street and remembered their first date together, how she'd reached for him through the darkness and fear that night.

He'd promised to protect her. From the publicity that had

ruined her life, from the memories that threatened to take the new one she'd built. He'd even tried to protect her from herself, slowing down her headlong rush to experience sex and life full force.

He hadn't protected her from a damn thing. Instead he'd led a small army of television crews right to her front door. Not to mention the fact that his obviously deranged father now held a gun to her head and threatened her life.

His stomach revolted at the image in his mind.

He'd promised to help her forget the single most devastating experience of her life. Instead, he'd brought her another one, one that might end the life she'd fought so hard to recover.

He would never forgive himself if something happened to her.

"She'll be fine. She's strong."

He looked up to find Anne standing above him, blocking out the drooping August sun. He hadn't realized just how hot he'd been until the cool patch of shade slid over him.

"And he's mental. I should be in there, it should be me. I've tried several times, but they're watching. I don't get more than five steps before some well-meaning police officer has my arm in one hand and a soda in the other. If she lives through this, I'll never drink another one again."

"You love her, don't you?"

He took a large sip from the watered-down cup in his hand, the swallow catching on the large lump permanently lodged in his throat.

"More than I ever thought possible. Not that it matters anymore."

He was going to lose her, too. He felt the sinking sensation straight through to the center of his bones. He'd watched as his mother wasted away, cancer eating her from the inside out.

Only, this time, instead of living with the thought that he hadn't been able to do anything to help his mother, he'd be living with the knowledge that he was directly responsible for Karyn's death.

16

KARYN STARED AT DARRELL as he paced through her living room. Her butt was numb from sitting on the wooden floor for the last several hours, her back pressed tightly to the wall. It didn't matter. She'd sit here forever if it meant he wouldn't point that gun at her again.

She'd honestly thought her life would end the moment he'd realized Chris had called the police. Darrell had stalked across the room, grabbed a handful of her hair and pressed the hard barrel of the gun to her head. He'd ground it against her skin— the spot still throbbed. But he hadn't pulled the trigger. Not at her. Instead, he'd shot several times through the front window. She didn't think he'd been aiming at the cops, but…

The more she watched him, the less certain she was that he could do it. Kill her.

Yes, the man had issues, but was he a murderer? She didn't think so. But she also wasn't ready to test the theory with her life.

Her stomach growled loudly. She ignored it.

"Damn it! I'm going to kill that bastard son of mine. All I wanted was what he owed me."

Karyn had listened to the same refrain most of the day. She still wasn't exactly sure what he thought was owed him, and she didn't want to find out. If she just sat quietly in the corner, he tended to ignore her.

He'd spoken several times on the phone. She supposed with

the police, maybe a negotiator. She didn't know for sure. At one time she'd heard him ask to speak to Chris, but she didn't think he had. She was beginning to hope he might have a stroke on her floor. He wasn't a young man, after all, and the vein in his neck bulged out farther than she thought humanly possible.

He mumbled to himself as he crossed back and forth in front of her. She watched his progress, never taking her eyes from the gun held firmly in his hand. If the opportunity presented itself…

The breath caught in her lungs as he swung suddenly to face her. He dropped onto his haunches in front of her, that menacing piece of black metal dangling between his open knees.

"What do you think?"

She swallowed through a dry throat. "About what?"

"I figure a few years in jail. Probably not worth killing myself over. Not like I actually hurt you or anything."

He stared at her with Chris's eyes and as she watched they took on a tight gleam. She recognized it as something akin to the desire Chris saw her with, only this had a sinister, manic tinge that set her skin crawling.

"What do you say?" He reached for her, running a finger over her cheek into the open vee of her T-shirt, caressing the top swell of her breast. She shivered in disgust, recognizing the cold edge of debilitating fear.

"I'll probably be going away for a while, why don't you give me something to remember?"

Her stomach clenched and she ground her teeth together, answering through them, "I don't think so." She would not show him the weakness of her underlying emotions.

His eyes narrowed and his lip curled up in a sneer. She couldn't believe that when he'd first walked into her apartment she'd thought him close to Chris in looks and mannerisms. This man was nothing like the one who'd done his best to help her.

Reaching beneath his shirt, Darrell pulled out something. From the back it looked to her like a torn piece of newsprint.

"Like son, like father, right? You've had the boy, now why not try a man?"

He flipped the photo into her lap. Her eyes left his long enough to watch it settle there. That was a mistake. She could have countered his assault—if she'd seen it coming.

Instead she was focused on a huge headline: Dr. Desire Accused of Misconduct in Relationship with Rape Victim Caller. Her stomach contracted then dropped about ten stories.

Before she could process the information, Darrell attacked her. His strong hands settled around her arms. Her heart thumped erratically, a band of fear constricting her chest. He jerked her sideways, trying to pull her flat to the floor. Her muscles tensed in automatic protest as she watched the paper fall through her legs to the floor.

And something snapped inside.

With every ounce of her strength, she kicked out as hard as she could.

The shock and the force sent him back a foot. His fingernails raked long trenches into her skin as he fell, trying hard to keep his grip.

She gathered her strength to kick again, but before she could connect with his chest, all hell broke loose.

People descended from everywhere, talking, yelling, falling on the man she'd just shoved away. She heard the unmistakable sound of flesh connecting with flesh. A yelp of pain and a metallic clink she assumed was handcuffs. It was a blur of motion she couldn't pull apart and all over in minutes, with not a single shot fired.

Someone—she had no idea who—bundled her into a blanket and whisked her away into the back of a waiting ambulance. She was minutes down the street when the shaking began, and she was thankful for the warm wool despite the August heat.

"THEY HAVE HER. She's fine." An officer rushed up beside them, spat out the words and then disappeared again.

Chris jumped from his perch on the curb and stared down the street. He barely had time to think before a flurry of activity caught his attention at the front door.

Karyn, whole, with no obvious signs of blood or trauma, was being rushed down her sidewalk to the ambulance that had been waiting off to the side the entire day. She had a blanket wrapped around her shoulders and an officer on either side, but she appeared to be moving under her own steam.

A pit opened up in the bottom of his stomach, and he fought back the sudden urge to vomit. She was alive. Right now that was enough.

He was across the barrier—this time no one tried to stop him—and reached the ambulance just as they closed the doors on her and roared away.

"Where are they taking her? Where is she going?" Chris looked around expectantly at the knot of people. They all ignored him, seeming to have more important things to occupy their attention.

There was nothing more important than her.

"Where are they taking her?" He roared at the top of his voice. A sudden silence fell over the people around him.

"Brookwood."

"Thank you." He spun on his heel, intending to jump in his car and head straight there as fast as the damn thing would go. But something stopped him. Another commotion at the front door.

His father was the first one through this time, his arms

pulled tight behind his back, several officers flanking the one who held the handcuffed hands.

Darrell seemed to zero in on him despite the people milling about. He sneered and made a move against the binding cuffs that prompted a quick jerk from the man holding him captive.

Chris saw red. He wanted to kill him.

"I wouldn't if I were you."

Anne's throaty voice stopped him.

"He isn't worth it."

She was right. But it still didn't help.

Karyn. She was what was important. He needed to get to her, make sure she was okay.

Somehow he made it to the hospital without being pulled over for a ticket. Any other time, he'd have been exhilarated to let the Porsche open up and fly. But that wasn't why his blood pumped ninety to nothing through his veins today.

He careened into the hospital, not caring that he'd taken a handicap spot. It was closest to the door and he'd damn well pay the fine.

With a sliding stop, he reached the nurses station. "Karyn Mitchell. Where is she?"

The nurse behind the opened glass looked him up and down, taking in the rumpled shirt and slacks he'd sweated through hours ago in the hot summer sun.

"Ms. Mitchell has asked for no visitors."

"But—"

"Unless your name is Anne, you're not wanted."

KARYN PUSHED HERSELF higher up on the sofa at Anne's duplex to get more comfortable. The tape over the gauze square on her arm pulled against her skin and the tiny hairs. With an exasperated sigh, she jerked the thing off. That hurt worse than the scratches did.

She supposed the emergency room staff had felt obligated to do something after keeping her there for several hours. They'd finally let her leave at around six o'clock after wrapping her arm. Her mom would have just used a couple of Band-Aids.

"Need anything?"

"Nope. Thanks for letting me stay tonight. I just wasn't ready to go home."

The thought of sleeping alone in her dark apartment had not been appealing. Neither had the constantly ringing phone or the swarm of people waiting outside for her when she'd stopped by to pick up some clothes.

"No problem. You know you're welcome to stay as long as you'd like."

She smiled up at her friend. It was a little shakier than she'd like, but it would get better.

"I'm fine. Honestly. I'm not hurt or even scarred for life. I'll get over it." Just not tonight.

Anne walked across her living room. Karyn had always thought the dark, dusky-rose carpet and the warm beige walls suited her friend to perfection. Only Anne could pull off this color scheme without it being too froufrou.

Her friend hit the switch on her stereo system just in time for Chris's voice to fill the room.

"I'd really rather not listen to his show tonight."

"You know he was there right? That he spent agonizing hours outside in the heat thinking he'd be responsible for your death."

"But he wasn't. So could you turn it off? Just for tonight?"

Yes, she'd known he was there, sitting vigil outside her house all day. She hadn't needed Anne to tell her that. She knew Chris, knew he would feel responsible for his father's actions. For bringing the man into her life.

Which was why she'd pushed him away. The nurses had thought she was stupid, not allowing Dr. Desire in to see her.

But he'd only come to assuage his guilt, to apologize once again for intruding on her life.

The only problem was she wanted him to intrude. Not because he fought guilt and a sense of responsibility, but because he loved her.

But he didn't. And she couldn't trust herself to see him and be strong enough to push him away again. It had nearly killed her to do it the first time. An ironic smile touched the corners of her mouth. In more ways than one.

She looked up at her friend, pleading. Anne's eyes narrowed into bright green slits. "No. No, I won't turn it off." She took the harshness of her words away with a gentle smile.

Dropping back onto the pillow stuffed behind her, Karyn rolled her head against the arm of the couch and stared up at the ceiling.

"You do realize it's over, right? I mean, it was only supposed to last for a few days, anyway. I was nothing more than a pet project to him. And I don't want another few days with him just because he feels guilty his father tried to kill me."

A launched throw pillow landed squarely on her chest. "You're so full of shit. I think you're just scared to open yourself up and let him in, only to get hurt."

Karyn tipped her head up and glared. "Hello, pot, I'm kettle."

Anne waved her hand and Karyn's words away. "We're not talking about me. We're talking about you. Do you love him?"

She dropped back down and closed her eyes. "Yes."

"Then you're an idiot. You've spent the past few years of your life afraid to take a chance, Karyn, afraid to make another mistake, to let yourself be vulnerable and get hurt."

So her friend was right. What did that change? Chris would break her heart. She was just limiting the pain.

"How's that working for you?"

"Up until Chris it was working just fine."

"Bullshit. Being sexually frustrated was so not working for you. He might hurt you—I don't think he will, but I can't promise you he won't. And neither can he for that matter. He might die in a car crash tomorrow. But wouldn't you hate yourself for missing today?"

Karyn glared over at her friend. "No, actually, I'd have been happy to miss today."

Anne walked to her, smoothed a cool hand over her forehead and brushed wisps of hair from her face.

"The pain's there, anyway, isn't it?"

She looked up into her friend's face and fought back tears. They'd both experienced their share of disappointment.

Before she could say anything, Anne walked away, leaving her alone with nothing but Chris's voice and the dark.

"Tonight we're starting the show a bit differently. I want to address what happened today. I will talk about this once, and only once, and never again. We will not be accepting any phone calls on the subject of Karyn, her past or what happened today."

The familiar shiver snaked down her spine as his voice filled the night around her. A part of her, a huge part, yearned to have him here, holding her tight.

"The powers that be want me to admit that I made a mistake to smooth everything over, as if saying I'm sorry will fix it all. It won't, partly because nothing will fix what happened to Karyn, but mostly because despite everything I can't regret what happened."

And neither could she. Yes, she'd been hurt, hearing his voice made the pain in her chest throb even harder. But Anne was right; spending the last few days with Chris had been amazing. She wouldn't trade them for anything, not even for the chance to erase today.

"I've spent the past five years talking about relationships, giving advice about sex, providing the male perspective on life and love. And I've been wrong. If I'm sorry about anything, it's that.

"I shouldn't have been giving anyone advice, because I had no idea what I was talking about—until I met Karyn."

Chris's words filtered through her pain. Her chest constricted with a band of hope that she tried desperately to cut herself free from. Hope only made it worse.

"She changed everything. She changed me. And I'm sorry for hurting her, for breaking a promise to her, for not protecting her when she'd entrusted me with more than her life, with her past, her soul and her secrets."

The band pulled tighter at her chest. Had she been wrong? Chris's words swirled in her brain. He certainly didn't sound like a man racked with guilt. Yes, it was there, but she also recognized the twin of her own pain in his words, in his voice.

"She asked me for one small thing, something that should have been easily given. And yet, I couldn't do it. For that I'm sorry.

"But I'm not sorry that we met. That she trusted me with a sexual experience that goes far beyond anything I've encountered before. I've never given everything of myself to anyone, I've never opened myself wholly. But she didn't hesitate—she trusted me enough to bare her soul and show me all she held inside.

"For *that* I am not sorry. I'm blessed."

Karyn's throat tingled and her eyes pricked with tears. Her lungs felt tight before that band finally burst and her heart swelled up to squeeze away space.

"I don't regret a single moment I spent with Karyn. I do regret that those moments were taken from her, tainted with something dark. And I regret that what happened was a direct result of my actions."

Karyn fumbled in the dark for her purse. Grabbing it from

the end table behind her head, she hit the door at a run, rummaging for her keys and cell.

"Dr. Desire show."

"Michael? It's Karyn. I want to talk to him. But not until I get to the station."

"Take line-three first."

Michael popped his head through the connecting door at the tail end of the second break. Chris dropped bonelessly into his chair and let his pounding head fall back. It would be a miracle if he got through this night.

The intro music played. He took a deep breath and prepared to fake his way through the show. Tomorrow he'd be sitting down with the station to discuss the future. It was a meeting he'd called. If they couldn't find a way for him to live comfortably with both Dr. Desire *and* his conscience then he'd simply leave and figure out something else to do with his life. Life was too short to be miserable. And suddenly the security this job offered wasn't as important as it used to be.

Maybe he'd go back to school.

"Welcome to the show. How can I help find that spark?"

"I have a question, Dr. Desire."

A jolt of electricity shot down his spine. Karyn.

His eyes flew to Michael's in the window. His producer had the biggest, smuggest smile he'd ever seen.

It was contagious.

"What's your question?"

"I was listening to your show last night, to the caller who asked about getting her boyfriend to commit."

Chris wanted to groan. He remembered that call.

"So, you don't think there's a way to reform men afraid to commit?"

He had no idea where Karyn was going with this… His heart

raced as he flipped the question over and over in his mind trying to figure it out. A sinking realization settled over him.

"Just last night, I said no, that women looking for commitment should steer clear of those men who are afraid of the word. But today something changed."

"Oh, yeah? What was that?"

"I realized I don't know what the hell I'm talking about." Her soft laugh echoed down the line and he wanted to yell his own joy.

"No, women shouldn't be unrealistic about their relationships, but they also shouldn't let a slick facade blind them against possibilities. Things can change. People can change."

"I'm really happy to hear that because I'm desperately in love with a man who is notorious for his reluctance to commit."

Chris swallowed past the lump in his throat at hearing her say the word. "Love?"

"Love."

"It changes everything. He has to fall in love."

"And *did* you?" she asked.

A soft hand landed on his shoulder.

One minute he'd been staring at the board in front of him, wishing he could wrap her in his arms. The next, she was there. So he did.

He shot up from his chair so fast the cord connecting his headphones practically jerked him back onto his ass. Throwing them to the floor, he crushed her to him before holding her away. His eyes raked every single inch, making sure she really was okay.

Once he was certain, he crushed his mouth to hers again with enough force to bruise. It didn't matter. She was here. Alive. With him.

With a shaky laugh she pulled back and asked, "*Did* you?"

"Did I what?"

"Fall in love."

"Absolutely."

Her eyes danced with happiness and mischief. He wanted nothing more than to spend the rest of his life making sure they always would.

"Promise me something."

"Anything."

"You'll burn that book the minute we get home."

"Book?"

"Yeah." A single eyebrow arched high, she stared at him with a knowing gleam. *"Sexual Abuse, Understanding and Recovery."*

He cringed.

"If you want…but why?"

"Because we don't need it. We never did." With a soft kiss to his lips, she whispered, "You're the only thing I ever needed, the only thing I ever will."

Epilogue

CHRIS PULLED HER beneath the surface of the lake. His hands trailed up her body from ankle to calf to thigh. One played rogue beneath her bathing suit as he pulled her face to his for an underwater kiss.

Surfacing minutes later, Karyn was light-headed from lack of oxygen and pleasantly giddy with desire.

Her gaze raked the shore, where her family had gathered to enjoy the long holiday weekend.

She was glad Chris had talked her into coming, into getting away. While the media frenzy had quickly died down, things were still a little crazy back in Birmingham.

At least they no longer had to worry about Darrell. At the moment he was rotting in some tiny little prison she hoped to God was very unpleasant. Even with everything that had happened, the man had still had the gall to ask Chris to post bail.

He'd delighted in declining.

She, on the other hand, had taken advantage of this trip to mend fences with her mother. Things were by no means perfect, but they were improving and that was all she could hope for. It would take time, but eventually they'd be fine. The fact that her mother approved of Karyn's choice in fiancés hadn't hurt, either.

Chris wrapped his arms around her waist, pulling her back into his chest and kicking them away to float together. She enjoyed the feel of him against her body—and the thick ridge nestled snugly at her back.

She angled her head and placed a kiss to the underside of his jaw.

Chris tipped them both back into the water, letting his hands graze over her breasts before settling at the juncture of her thighs. A gasp stuck in her throat as a single finger slipped deep inside.

"Chris."

Karyn jerked her head toward her family, all lined up on the beach, drinking, laughing, splashing in the shallows.

"They can't see. Trust me."

She did, with every last shred of herself. She knew with Chris she'd always be safe. But for both of them, safety was no longer what was most important. They had learned love would always be stronger than the fear.

* * * * *

The Colton family is back!
Enjoy a sneak preview of
COLTON'S SECRET SERVICE
by Marie Ferrarella,
part of THE COLTONS: FAMILY FIRST *miniseries.*

Available from Silhouette Romantic Suspense
in September 2008

He cautioned himself to be leery. He was human and he'd been conned before. But never by anyone nearly so attractive. Never by anyone he'd felt so attracted to.

In her defense, Nick supposed that Georgie could actually be telling him the truth. That she was a victim in all this. He had his people back in California checking her out, to make sure she was who she said she was and had, as she claimed, not even been near a computer, but on the road these last few months that the threats had been made.

In the meantime, he was doing his own checking out. Up close and exceedingly personal. So personal he could feel his blood stirring.

It had been a long time since he'd thought of himself as anything other than a law enforcement agent of one type or other. But Georgeann Grady made him remember that beneath the oaths he had taken and his devotion to duty, there beat the heart of a man.

A man who'd been far too long without the touch of a woman.

He watched as the light from the fireplace caressed the outline of Georgie's small, trim, jean-clad body as she moved about the rustic living room that could have easily come off the set of a Hollywood Western. Except that it was genuine.

As genuine as she claimed to be?

Something inside of him hoped so.

He wasn't supposed to be taking sides. His only interest in being here was to guarantee Senator Joe Colton's safety as the latter continued to make his bid for the presidency. Everything else was supposed to be secondary, but, Nick had to silently admit, that was just a wee bit hard to remember right now.

Earlier, before she'd put her precocious handful of a daughter to bed, Georgie had fed his appetite by whipping up some kind of a delicious concoction out of the vegetables she'd pulled from her garden. Vegetables that, by all rights, should have been withered and dried. She'd mentioned that a friend came by on occasion to weed and tend it. Still, it surprised him that somehow she'd managed to make something mouthwatering out of it.

Almost as mouthwatering as she looked to him right at this moment.

Again, he was reminded of the appetite that hadn't been fed, hadn't been satisfied.

And wasn't going to be, Nick sternly told himself. At least not now. Maybe later, when things took on a more definite shape and all the questions in his head were answered to his satisfaction, there would be time to explore this feeling. This woman. But not now.

Damn it.

"Sorry about the lack of light," Georgie said, breaking into his train of thought as she turned around to face him. If she noticed the way he was looking at her, she gave no indication. "But I don't see a point in paying for electricity if I'm not going to be here. Besides, Emmie really enjoys camping out. She likes roughing it."

"And you?" Nick asked, moving closer to her, so close that a whisper would have trouble fitting in. "What do you like?"

The very breath stopped in Georgie's throat as she looked up at him.

"I think you've got a fair shot of guessing that one," she told him softly.

* * * * *

Be sure to look for COLTON'S SECRET SERVICE
and the other following titles from
THE COLTONS: FAMILY FIRST *miniseries:*
RANCHER'S REDEMPTION by Beth Cornelison
THE SHERIFF'S AMNESIAC BRIDE by Linda Conrad
SOLDIER'S SECRET CHILD by Caridad Piñeiro
BABY'S WATCH by Justine Davis
A HERO OF HER OWN by Carla Cassidy

Silhouette

Desire

Silhouette Desire

Gifts from a Billionaire

JOAN HOHL

THE M.D.'S MISTRESS

Dr. Rebecca Jameson collapses from
exhaustion while working at a remote
African hospital. Fellow doctor Seth Andrews
ships her back to America so she can heal.
Rebecca is finally with the sexy surgeon
she's always loved. But would their affair
last longer than the week?

**Available September
wherever books are sold.**

Always Powerful, Passionate and Provocative.

Inside ROMANCE

Stay up-to-date on all your romance reading news!

The Inside Romance newsletter is a FREE quarterly newsletter highlighting our upcoming series releases and promotions!

Click on the <u>Inside Romance</u> link on the front page of **www.eHarlequin.com** or e-mail us at insideromance@harlequin.ca to sign up to receive your FREE newsletter today!

You can also subscribe by writing us at: HARLEQUIN BOOKS Attention: Customer Service Department P.O. Box 9057, Buffalo, NY 14269-9057

Please allow 4-6 weeks for delivery of the first issue by mail.

IRNIBPA208

REQUEST YOUR FREE BOOKS!

2 FREE NOVELS
PLUS 2
FREE GIFTS!

HARLEQUIN®

Blaze™

Red-hot reads!

YES! Please send me 2 FREE Harlequin® Blaze™ novels and my 2 FREE gifts (gifts are worth about $10). After receiving them, if I don't wish to receive any more books, I can return the shipping statement marked "cancel". If I don't cancel, I will receive 6 brand-new novels every month and be billed just $4.24 per book in the U.S. or $4.71 per book in Canada, plus 25¢ shipping and handling per book and applicable taxes, if any*. That's a savings of 15% or more off the cover price! I understand that accepting the 2 free books and gifts places me under no obligation to buy anything. I can always return a shipment and cancel at any time. Even if I never buy another book, the two free books and gifts are mine to keep forever.

151 HDN ERVA 351 HDN ERUX

Name	(PLEASE PRINT)	
Address		Apt. #
City	State/Prov.	Zip/Postal Code

Signature (if under 18, a parent or guardian must sign)

Mail to the **Harlequin Reader Service:**
IN U.S.A.: P.O. Box 1867, Buffalo, NY 14240-1867
IN CANADA: P.O. Box 609, Fort Erie, Ontario L2A 5X3

Not valid to current subscribers of Harlequin Blaze books.

Want to try two free books from another line?
Call 1-800-873-8635 or visit www.morefreebooks.com.

* Terms and prices subject to change without notice. N.Y. residents add applicable sales tax. Canadian residents will be charged applicable provincial taxes and GST. Offer not valid in Quebec. This offer is limited to one order per household. All orders subject to approval. Credit or debit balances in a customer's account(s) may be offset by any other outstanding balance owed by or to the customer. Please allow 4 to 6 weeks for delivery. Offer available while quantities last.

Your Privacy: Harlequin Books is committed to protecting your privacy. Our Privacy Policy is available online at www.eHarlequin.com or upon request from the Reader Service. From time to time we make our lists of customers available to reputable third parties who may have a product or service of interest to you. If you would prefer we not share your name and address, please check here. ☐

HB08R

▼ *Silhouette*®

SPECIAL EDITION™

NEW YORK TIMES
BESTSELLING AUTHOR

DIANA PALMER

A brand-new Long, Tall Texans novel

HEART OF STONE

Feeling unwanted and unloved, Keely returns
to Jacobsville and to Boone Sinclair, a rancher
troubled by his own past. Boone has always
seemed reserved, but now Keely discovers a
sensuality with him that quickly turns to love. Can
they each see past their own scars to let love in?

*Available September 2008
wherever you buy books.*

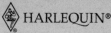

HARLEQUIN®

Blaze™

COMING NEXT MONTH

#417 ALL OR NOTHING Debbi Rawlins
Posing undercover as a Hollywood producer to investigate thefts at the
St. Martine hotel has good ol' Texas cowboy Chase Culver sweatin' under
his Stetson. All the up-close contact with the hotel's gorgeous personal trainer
Dana McGuire isn't helping either, and she's his prime suspect!

#418 RISQUÉ BUSINESS Tawny Weber
Blush
Delaney Connor can't believe the way her life has changed! The former mousy
college professor is now a TV celebrity, thanks to a makeover and a talent for
reviewing pop fiction. She's at the top of her game—until bad boy author
Nick Angel tests her skills both as a reviewer…and as a woman.

#419 AT HER PLEASURE Cindi Myers
Who knew science could be so…sensual? For researcher Ian Marshall his
summer of solitude on an uninhabited desert island becomes much more
interesting with the arrival of Nicole Howard. And when she offers a no-
strings-attached affair, how can he resist?

#420 SEX & THE SINGLE SEAL Jamie Sobrato
Forbidden Fantasies
When something feels this taboo, it has to be right. That's how Lieutenant
Commander Kyle Thomas explains her against-the-rules lust for her
subordinate Drew MacLeod. So when she finally gets the chance to seduce
him, nothing will stand in her way.

#421 LIVE AND YEARN Kelley St. John
The Sexth Sense, Bk. 6
When Charles Roussel runs into former flame Nanette Vicknair, he knows
she's still mad at his betrayal years ago. But before he can explain, he's cast
adrift in a nether world, neither alive nor dead. Except, that is, in her bed every
night. There he proves to her that he's truly the man of her dreams!

#422 OVERNIGHT SENSATION Karen Foley
Actress Ivy James has just hit the big time. She's earned the lead role in a
blockbuster movie based on the true-to-life sexual experiences of war hero
Garrett Stokes, and her costar is one of Hollywood's biggest and brightest
actors. The problem? The only one she wants to share a bed with—on-screen
and off—is Garrett himself!